THE AUTHOR

John Hampson Simpson was born in Birmingham in 1901. His family made its name in the Midlands through the theatre and the brewing industry, but a business collapse meant that John grew up in poverty. Always in weak health, he was educated at home and, after the 1914-18 War, (part of which he spent in a munitions factory), he took a variety of jobs – from billiard marker to chef – in Nottingham, London, Derby and elsewhere. In 1925 he settled down as a tutor to a mentally handicapped boy in Dorridge, near Birmingham, and there he began to write.

Saturday Night at the Greyhound, Hampson's first book, was an immediate success when published by The Hogarth Press in 1931, and was followed by *O Providence* (1932), *Strip Jack Naked* (1934), *Family Curse* (1936), and *Care of 'The Grand'* (1939). In the Thirties he became the leading figure in the so-called Birmingham Group, which included Walter Allen, Walter Brierley, Leslie Halward and Peter Chamberlain. Other literary friends were Forrest Reid, William Plomer, Graham Greene, Louis MacNeice and W. H. Auden, who, having set the lead himself, cajoled Hampson into a marriage of convenience to provide a British passport for the German actress Thérèse Giehse in 1936. During the war he wrote documentaries for the BBC, through which he became interested in the ideas of the psychologist James Ford Thomson, whom he visited in India in 1948, and to whom he dedicated his last novel, *A Bag of Stones* (1952). A solitary man, introverted and gentle, John Hampson died in Solihull in 1955.

SATURDAY NIGHT AT THE GREYHOUND

John Hampson

*New Introduction by
Christopher Hawtree*

THE HOGARTH PRESS
LONDON

To
FORREST REID

WITH GRATITUDE

Published in 1986 by
The Hogarth Press
Chatto & Windus Ltd
40 William IV Street, London WC2N 4DF

First published in Great Britain by The Hogarth Press 1931
This edition offset from Eyre & Spottiswoode 1950 edition
Copyright John Hampson
Introduction copyright © Christopher Hawtree 1986

All rights reserved. No part of this publication may be reproduced, stored in a retrieval system, or transmitted in any form, or by any means, electronic, mechanical, photocopying, recording or otherwise, without the prior permission of the publisher.

British Library Cataloguing in Publication Data

Hampson, John
Saturday night at the Greyhound.
I. Title
823'.912[F]   PR6058.A554/

ISBN 0 7012 0652 7

Printed in Great Britain by
Cox & Wyman Ltd
Reading, Berkshire

INTRODUCTION

On his death at the end of 1955, John Hampson was given an obituary of two inches in *The Times*. As an indication both of the obscurity in which he chose to live and of a post-war shift in literary fashion such paucity could hardly be bettered. Twenty-five years earlier, *Saturday Night at the Greyhound*, along with *Orlando* and *The Edwardians*, had been one of The Hogarth Press's biggest sellers. Far removed from those two, it is Hampson's finest novel, one whose stark prose, reflecting a grim world, set it at the head of a now-neglected regional movement in English fiction during the 1930s. 'One has no great hopes from Birmingham. I always say there is something direful in the sound,' remarks Mrs. Elton in *Emma*. Prolonged observation led these Midlands writers to much the same conclusion.

Born in 1901, John Hampson was the fifth of eight children. His parents – Kathleen and Mercer Hampson Simpson – belonged to a strong artistic and theatrical tradition, which had developed when his great-grandfather ran away from Nottingham to become an actor and, eventually, in 1837, the manager of Birmingham's Theatre Royal. An acute and diverse financial sense ensured the family's prosperity in the nineteenth century and enabled the young, delicate Hampson to be all but pampered. With the sudden collapse of the brewing business at Aston, Hampson's father had to forfeit any inheritance, and in these reduced circumstances the family moved to Leicester, where, after a struggle, he managed to find work as the manager of a motor-cycle depot; one of Hampson's brothers, Jimmy, was to become famous as a racing-cyclist.

The overhanging sense of poverty heightened the family conflicts – ones that were made all the greater because the demands of each member's practical and artistic sides had been frustratingly divided in this adversity. Their father's essentially humane nature was now punctuated by violent rages, which perhaps led to a somewhat masochistic streak in his son, whose novels contain a high proportion of beatings at the hands of ill-adjusted fathers while the wife looks on hopelessly. Kept by his health from attending the village school, Hampson stayed at home, with the result that a sense that he lacked any formal education needlessly dogged him for the rest of his life. This state of affairs increased the closeness he felt towards his sister Mona, and such emotional turbulence was further complicated by his developing homosexuality, something which, if an early unpublished novel is an accurate record, was brought out by an encounter, ironically enough, with a wayward schoolmaster.

In writing to him about his final novel, William Plomer noted that 'here again I think I perceive your prevalent theme of the secret enemy of society – with, always, I think, the implication that he *needn't* have been, if only society were better behaved'. Hampson himself, the family dispersed during the Great War, despaired of his work in a munitions factory and, in his turn, left to find work in Nottingham. For some years he worked in many odd, casual ways, some of which would be reflected in his fiction: as a kitchen-hand, a billiard marker, a commis waiter, a waiter in a London hotel, a chef in Derby – and at one point he was summoned to join his sister as 'part-protection' in running a pub in the North Derbyshire village of Ashover. Desperation also caused him to turn to book-thieving and one volume too many of Gray's *Anatomy* brought him a time in Wormwood Scrubs, something he was always especially eager to conceal. (Cyril Connolly, of course, was never caught.)

In 1925, having returned to the family home, he found work as a nurse and companion to a mongol child, Ronald Wilson, whose parents and sister lived at Four Ashes, an Elizabethan country house at Dorridge, some seven miles from Birmingham. As Graham Greene has written, he grew very much to love his charge 'and was invaluable to the moron's parents. He really sacrificed his life to this task.' The security and stability of life with the Wilsons none the less allowed him, over the next few years, to set about the catharsis of writing to which his upbringing and chequered life had driven him.

By enviable dint of waking early and writing before the day's main work began, he was able to complete a number of works in the late Twenties. The first of these was *Saturday Night at the Greyhound*, which drew upon an incident during his time at the Ashover pub with his sister. (Curiously enough, the same obscure pub a few years on figures, unnamed, in *A Sort of Life*, where it proved to be an unsatisfactory refuge during Graham Greene's brief, early stretch as a tutor to the son of a widow.) In its original form, Hampson's work took the shape of a three-act play written for his brother's amateur dramatic group in Derby. It was later rewritten as a novel 'on the rebound' of rejection by more august theatrical companies, as he remarked to Jonathan Cape, whose publishing house also turned him down. In the meanwhile he had begun *O Providence*, on which he was to work for four years, as well as the unpublished *Tuneless Numbers*, some stories and *Go Seek a Stranger*. With this welling up of fiction, he began to look further for a publisher. *Go Seek a Stranger* reached Leonard Woolf, who was distinctly encouraging but wary of taking a novel with a predominantly homosexual theme. By this time Hampson, urged on by Forrest Reid, had also completed both *Saturday Night at the Greyhound* and *O Providence*, both of which were now accepted by Leonard Woolf.

Saturday Night at the Greyhound was published in February 1931 and was immediately and widely praised: a piece by Harold Nicolson for the *Daily Express* in particular helped to propel it through two reprints in the space of ten days. Later reissued by Heinemann, it was also an early, successful Penguin and was translated into French by *La Nouvelle Revue Française*. Despite all this, he did not have any luck in persuading Beatrix Lehmann to take part in a stage version, and discussions with Alec Bristow about a film version came to nothing.

'The style at first appears harsh, even crude,' wrote Walter Allen of his work in *Tradition and Dream*. 'It is in fact the natural expression of an abhorrence of anything like fine writing or verbal decoration or the obviously charming. Its angularity reflects the angularity of a mind intransigently honest, not cynical but unillusioned and sardonic, stoic.' Although the visit by an upper-class, week-ending girl who is weary of hotel-life and the elaborations of *Sodome et Gomorrhe* and *Prancing Nigger* somewhat disturbs the intense, almost chamber-like nature of the family drama in *Saturday Night at the Greyhound*, the novel draws its considerable power from the way in which it brings together so many of the concerns of Hampson's own life. (Robert Graves, author of a pamphlet about swearing, none the less delighted in the section where the girl walks along an ill-lit 'stone-flagged passage. It was going to be too dreadful. Carelessly she bumped into an unseen figure. Flippantly she called over her shoulder, "Sorrow." A man's voice answered harshly indignant, "And sod you too, you ignorant bitch." ') By putting so much of what he had experienced into the book's brief time-span, whose pace is accelerated by the curt style, Hampson was able to show with hideous plausibility how the night's remorseless sequence of events had their diverse origins in circumstances and conditions that go back not only months, but years. Walter Allen points to a 'bedrock quality' in the prose, and yet *Saturday Night at the Greyhound*, almost devoid of metaphor in itself, becomes a symbol of life as experienced by far more people than those who happened to cross the threshold that bleak evening.

A year later, *O Providence*, the second and last of his books to be published by the Woolfs, was less successful. 'Perhaps, as a whole, I should put it below *Saturday Night*,' E. M. Forster told him. Another of the writers whose acquaintance he made with the first novel's success, William Plomer, wrote him a long letter about *O Providence*, in the course of which he pointed to something which prevents so much of Hampson's writing from being fully realized:

The whole thing seems to me interesting as a case-history rather than as a work of literature. It may seem an absurd thing to say, but I don't think you are quite 'literary' enough. Nobody dislikes more than I do the sort of 'fine writing' and pretentiousness which abounds in these days, but I think you are inclined to go to another extreme, and write in a fashion too unadorned. This is all right, no doubt, in a book like the *Greyhound*, which depends so much on its quick and complex dramatic interest . . . but in a long novel I do not think it is safe to rely on such a manner of writing. For you are deliberately limiting, if not actually handicapping yourself. For example, by continually writing short unconnected sentences you prevent any long rhythms. You want to be staccato all the time, and that is fair neither to yourself or your audience.

Plomer, saying that Hampson took the reader along an interesting road but one of cobblestones not asphalt or grass, remarked that 'irony is the salt of the novel, and would add savour to many a passage in this book which is too coldly realistic'. It was advice that would later, after *Strip Jack Naked*, result in 1936's *Family Curse* (a punning title which summarizes much of Hampson), where he manages to tell the same story from each member's viewpoint without wearying the reader in the process. The ending of this complex novel is a triumphantly ironic victory for its customary 'secret enemy', a weak, artistic younger son, and *Family Curse* is much the most effective of Hampson's novels after *Saturday Night at the Greyhound*, although a brief, chilling story, 'The Sight of Blood', variously published in the Thirties, should also be sought out. 'You'll have to face a constricted as well as a restricted sale of the book, I'm sure,' wrote Forster to him of *Family Curse*. 'There's bound to be opposition to it. What it *will* do, is greatly to strengthen your reputation amongst people whose opinion you may probably value.'

In 1933 Hampson had completed the unpublished *Foreign English*, which anticipated fashion with its Berlin setting and homosexual entanglement. On a subsequent visit to the city he met the American ambassador's daughter, Miss Martha Dodd, who had reviewed his work, and with whom he now had a rather unexpected love affair. In the same year he met Walter Allen, who had studied at Birmingham University, and that meeting in its turn provided contact with such diverse characters as Auden, MacNeice, Reggie Smith and George Painter, all of whom had a connection, in one way or another, with the

University.

At about the same time, links developed between a number of Midlands writers after an American editor, Edward O'Brien, whose sense of English geography was as erratic as his enthusiasm for the short story was reckless, noticed that he was receiving a number of Midlands writers among his contributions and, assuming that they must all know one another, duly christened them the Birmingham Group. 'We never regarded ourselves as a group,' wrote Leslie Halward, whom Walter Allen has likened to Chekhov with more justice than the comparison usually merits. 'We were simply four young men who, having common interests and vaguely similar ideas, met periodically for the purpose of explaining to the other where he was wrong.'

Another of the four visitors to the pub off Corporation Street, a venue to which O'Brien's introductions had drawn them, was the short-story writer and novelist Peter Chamberlain, a friend of Hampson's motor-cycling brother. Less frequent were the appearances of Walter Brierley. His first novel was the excellent *Means-Test Man*, whose progress in manuscript, developed from Hampson's idea, was so closely followed by both Allen and Hampson as almost to be a collaboration. Sadly, his later work, lacking such guidance, sprawled along similar themes but never had the pace which makes the first novel an effective, disinterested account of the indignities of unemployment.

Hampson's horror of Fascism and the rise of the Nazis brought about a morning's event in 1936 which again shows his abundant good nature and which, owing to Auden's involvement, was one that became increasingly comic. Auden, having married Thomas Mann's daughter, Erika, so that she could flee Germany, was keen that the same should be done for her friend, the actress Thérèse Giehse (who died in 1975). 'What are buggers for?' he demanded irresistibly. A summary can hardly do full justice to this Solihull registry-office ceremony, with Auden in imperious command, the registrar struggling to cope with the literary gathering before him. While weddings often bring together families who do not know each other, it is an unusual situation for the bride and groom to be in, and to be estranged even further by their inability to speak each other's language, a predicament shared not only by the registrar but also by most of the others present. Auden's instructions to everyone concerned only added to the confusion. Elated by his success, and armed with a good supply of Thomas Mann's money, he then led the party to a nearby pub to celebrate, where, fortified with brandy, he was eager to play the piano. Ignoring the barmaid's incomprehensible expostulations, he marched to the billiard room, where his party was greeted by the sight of a corpse stretched out on the table. 'An occasion when Wystan was not allowed to play *Hymns Ancient and Modern*,' observes Walter Allen, who used jocularly to vie with Louis MacNeice over the literary rights in Hampson's wedding. His eventual account, in *As I Walked Down New Grub Street*, is a masterpiece of comedy.

Towards the end of the Thirties, Hampson, annoyed by the vogue for novels of hotel life which were so far removed from his own experience, published *Care of 'The Grand'* (Forster's title) in which again he provided a multiple perspective, one which brings out the double meaning of the title. Such architectural skill worked to less effect than it had done with the more cohesive elements of *Family Curse*. With the arrival of war he wrote *Poor Fancy Riches*, an unpublished fantasy novel well out of his range, and then, perhaps in search of a subject, he rather surprisingly tried for the RAF. The documentary nature of the hotel novel suggested that he would be better off in writing for the BBC. (He also wrote an entertaining volume on *The English at Table* for W. J. Turner's 'Britain in Pictures' series. 'I wish you would do two others,' remarked Forster. '*The English in the Bed*, and *The English on the Stool*.')

The BBC commissions led to his studying the work of James Ford Thomson, the eccentric and tiresome educational psychologist for Madras State. In 1948, with an advance from Eyre and Spottiswoode for a new edition of *Saturday Night at the Greyhound*, which Graham Greene was eager to include in his Century Library, Hampson went on a three-month Indian lecture tour, in the course of which he became a disciple of Thomson's, about whom he then wrote a long, unpublished book and to whom he dedicated his last novel, *A Bag of Stones*.

In the meanwhile, owing to post-war problems with paper supply, the Century Library had been slowed down and was further held up when Greene left the firm. 'I don't give up hope,' said William Plomer, 'and I hope that before the crematorium opens its jaws at us we may be allowed to see *Saturday Night* in its new form.' It did reappear, but a new plan to film it fell through after disagreements with the script writers, and, his health worsening with the Wilsons' move to Solihull, Hampson had returned to work on a stage version just when he was admitted to hospital.

Irritated by the noise of the Christmas festivities in the ward, he wilfully decided to discharge himself. As he dressed to leave he fell to the floor and died.

'His career had such a fair, and strange, start,' Forster had said to William Plomer a few years earlier ' . . . but he has not kept up as I hoped; too good and unselfish perhaps.' The first novel, which he had begun with the hope of a dramatic success similar to that which had brought his family to Victorian prominence, remained his best-known work in a varied and always interesting career which was so largely devoted to analysing the self-perpetuating misery with which providence can infect any household. His past was always with him.

Now, after so many years of distinct 'underground' popularity, the novel's classic status is as certain as its reissue is overdue. It reappears, not as a memorial, but as a work whose beguiling and direful sound is independent of any introductory essay.

Christopher Hawtree, Newbold Heath 1985

Note

I am very grateful to John Hampson's nephew and cousin, Roger Hubank and Mercer Simpson, for their help in preparing this introduction, and also to the Estates of E. M. Forster and William Plomer for permission to quote from unpublished letters.

CONTENTS

PART ONE

NIGHTFALL AT THE GREYHOUND — 17

PART TWO

THE OPEN HOUSE — 67

PART THREE

THE HOUSE CLOSES — 117

We rest—a dream has power to poison sleep;
We rise—one wandering thought pollutes the day;
We feel, conceive, or reason, laugh or weep,
Embrace fond woe, or cast our cares away.
                                        SHELLEY.

PART ONE
NIGHTFALL AT THE GREYHOUND

I

MRS. TAPIN sat by the kitchen fireplace. Soon, she knew, it would be four o'clock. For another half an hour she could sit close to the kitchen fire and think. Mrs. Tapin had no use for books; they only told of soft people who did not exist. Mrs. Tapin loved four things —money, gossip, thinking, and Clara. She did not worry about any of these four things though; whatever happened was food for thought. Of her own foresight she was proud, for things nearly always happened as she expected them to. These folks here now. The landlord, the landlord's wife, and her brother. Mrs. Tapin chuckled grimly: she had seen fourteen men take over the Greyhound Inn in her time. Fourteen, and none of them had made it pay. Scarcely kept them with food in their bellies, let alone clothes on their backs. Even old Dakin, who tried to farm the seven poor acres of land, had had to admit defeat and clear out, broken. The Skelt family, too. They fled on a pitch-black night, leaving chaos in the house; owing everyone money. The owning brewers had only just saved the licence that time. Mrs. Tapin giggled at the remembrance. Life was like that, always playing tricks. A sense of the funny side made life interesting. That the present landlord, a drunken townsman of shady repute, expected to make a living, and more, out of the Grovelace villagers, amused Mrs. Tapin splendidly. But she kept her joy secret. Fools believe in their folly, and expect others to do the same.

For many reasons Mrs. Tapin encouraged the landlord, Fred Flack, to think himself wise. There was only one thing she herself held against him: he was too free with Clara. Far too free. That must stop. After all, he could not make an honest woman of Clara as the old Squire had made an honest woman of herself. Tapin had not liked taking her much. But it had been either that or get out of his comfortable gamekeeper's cottage. The future held no store for a penniless man of sixty, as Tapin had been when he married her. Squire gave them twenty-five golden pounds. In spite of that, Tapin had never been able to like Clara. He was a silly old fool. She had managed him a treat. A threat to tell the rest of the village of the Squire's bargain soon brought him to heel. The daft old fool. As if the villagers, one and all, did not know all that was to be known of her affair with the Squire. Besides, as if anyone would believe an old dotard like Asa Tapin could have fathered her Clara. A more ladylike, finicking girl never trod the lanes of Grovelace village. Clara knew about it too, but not from legitimate sources. Mrs. Tapin was too cautious to confess the lapse to her own daughter. It might put extra fine ideas in the girl's head.

Clara might give herself more airs and graces, knowing herself to be the late Squire's bastard, but it would lead to no good if the present Squire heard of her mother's admitting the fact. Mrs. Tapin held no wish to be turned out of the gamekeeper's cottage at her time of life.

She made up the fire, then routed about in the larder for something to eat. Saturday was bad for food at the Greyhound. All she could take safely was a hunch of bread and cheese. She covered the bread thickly with butter and returned to her seat at the fireside, munching greedily. A tankard of the dark, nutty ale would have been nice. But the cellar head door was locked, and the bar parlour too. Landlady's brother, young Tom Oakley, slept with the keys under his pillow. Mrs. Tapin did not like young Tom. He was the nasty, suspicious sort. Always on the whine. No manner of hints ever drew a free half-pint of beer from him; too sharp he was, but not for Mrs. Tapin. She knew a thing or two about him, and what she did not know she could guess. Dirty little swipe. Who did he think he was to grouse at Clara's ways? As if Clara's own mother was not the person to speak, if speaking there was to be. Only half a man; the little shrimp. Mrs. Tapin liked a man to be a man, not an oily-headed, fancy-socked little snot. If he caught her eating the scrap of food he would tell his sister. The thought made Mrs. Tapin bolt the last mouthful hurriedly. She was not scared of Mrs. Flack, but she liked to preserve an appearance of strict honesty. It made her daily inroads on the house's stock less likely to be noticed. Young Tom suspected her, she thought, but then he was the sort who'd suspect anyone. Besides, Ivy Flack deserved to lose her things, she was that careless. Every Wednesday Mrs. Tapin returned the week's washing short of one article at least. The only time it had been noticed was when she kept back one of young Tom's shirts. That had been a silly thing to do; she had thought so at the time, and all but retraced her steps for it. Mrs. Flack had been busy, so she let it go. Next morning young Tom said, "You sent me back a shirt short. What about it?" Very quick she answered with a smile, "It dropped off basket in muck, Mister. Shall bring it to-morrow." That comforted him, though he stared. Mrs. Tapin giggled. Next week for spite she kept back a pillow-case and glass-cloth, but the soft, soppy Ivy did not miss them. That's what Clara called her. Soppy Ivy, but not so soft, Mrs. Tapin knew, not so soft, as Clara would find if Ivy caught her fooling about with the landlord. Soppy about him, but not soft. Mrs. Tapin had listened with great enjoyment to Ivy bitterly reproaching her husband for drinking too much. Ivy might be worse, but young Tom could not be. Blasted little swine. If he got his way neither she nor Clara would ever take another penny-piece in wages out of the house. "Keep the work amongst us, where the interest is," was what he said.

Landlord was not so fond of work, nor the Missus neither, which was something to be grateful for.

Mrs. Tapin drew a crumpled green packet from the hole in the side of her skirt. She enjoyed a cigarette. It allowed thought to run freely. Besides, Clara kept her well supplied from the bar stock. Only Clara and Ivy knew she smoked. Did not do to tell everyone everything. Most folks knew far too much as it was. What with Ma Pilly and Widow Hacks hinting about Clara and the landlord. By no manner of thinking could the landlord be of much use to Clara. When he left the Greyhound, as he would sooner or later, it would be with less money than when he took over six months ago. He was a drunkard too, a liar, and one who made free with any woman who would stand him. No use to Clara, whichever way he was looked at. Mrs. Tapin looked at every point from every side. That he had a wife ought to make Clara think before she allowed him any liberties. Girls were silly like: she had best have it out with Clara and no blasted nonsense either.

Clara was not a mug. She possessed a sly head on her shoulders. If Ivy did not suspect where the girl's champagne shoes and pink satin jumper came from, Mrs. Tapin did. Mrs. Tapin liked Clara's guile. It was worthy of her own skill. She had always been clever with men herself. Though it took five years to get the old Squire after her. But she had done it and got a husband into the bargain. Times had changed; the men were not so easy as they used to be. Mrs. Tapin sighed regretfully. It was a pity Clara never got a chance with the new young Squire. He was a gay one from all she heard. But he only came to Grovelace for the shooting. Brought fancy London pieces with him too. The damned motor-cars were the ruin of country life. People got too much choice; they saw too much. That was a mistake.

Mrs. Tapin threw the stub of her cigarette into the fire, and got to her feet. Quickly she cleared the dirty crocks from off the table into the sink. She worked deftly and at speed, making very little noise. In ten minutes the last plate was wiped and put away. She swept the floor, taking up the old rag rug, shaking it in the yard outside. When everything was straight indoors, she went out to the hen-house, stealing an egg from every nest. These she hid in the hedgerow. They could be collected later on her way home. She and old Asa both liked an egg to their breakfast. On her return to the dark kitchen, she trod accidentally on the paw of a greyhound that lay in front of the warm fire. Skilfully the dog nipped her ankle. She gazed at him, hatred in her eyes, and swung her foot, but the animal snarled in warning.

Mrs. Tapin hated all dogs: they won too much attention from the men. She had known old Asa sit up all night with a sick whippet, but she herself might lie in bed and rot before he would do anything for her.

The dog was handsome, his head long and narrow, the eyes bright and intelligent.

Mrs. Tapin was scared of him. She would like to kill him. A piece of clothes-line tied round his muscular neck would do the trick. She would do it, but not now;

later. Going into the pantry, she cut an inch-wide strip off the raw joint of beef, that wiped over Asa's pet hare would tempt the dog. She wrapped the meat in a scrap of rag, and slid it into her pocket, returning to her place by the fireside.

Winter would soon be over. She was sorry for that; the dark months were the best. People did not see so much; they had less chance of spying on her and Clara.

In all the fifty years she had lived in Grovelace, the place scarcely altered—not a house put up, nor yet one pulled down. Though plenty were falling, a brick at a time, into ruin. People, especially the young ones, got a much better time of things now, what with dancing offered at Scrutton every Saturday night, and pictures on at Chesterfield, six nights out of seven. Times were soft, people were getting the same; it made Mrs. Tapin sick. She believed in hard times for children; it taught them how to take care of themselves.

Clara was an exception. There was not a cottage girl for miles around who could hold a candle to her. She was fine-looking, clever. At school she had always won the good-conduct prize as well as one for arithmetic. Of course, she was different, and hardly a cottage child, with old Squire Grovedon as her father.

There were other Grovedon bastards in the place, but they kept their illegitimacy. Clara had been made proper by wedlock, so folks might talk till their tongues dropped off. Mrs. Tapin treasured all the precious papers locked away in a drawer; anyone who wished to see might. The papers were her pride; she never tired of boasting of them to less fortunate women of Squire Grovedon's choice. He had done more for her than he had for them, quite rightly too. It had been due to her as a tenant farmer's daughter. The other women were not of much account; they had deserved all they got. She knew what the reward of her alliance with the Squire would be, long before she attracted him.

After living thirty years of life, unmarried, working early mornings and late at night on the farm, helping to rear the younger children, she got tired of being a maid.

No suitable young farmer turned up to woo her; marry a miner she would not, though two asked for her. Better by far be an old man's bride. She had made a mistake about Asa: of the list Squire proposed she might choose from he was the oldest by ten years. Of the three others, one was a stable-man, a lad of her own age; she had been tempted, but the boy's nasty temper dissuaded her. In taking Asa, an ex-head gamekeeper with a nice little pension, she considered his age a great attraction.

But he still hung on to life, the old wretch; she was sure he did it out of spite. What was the use of him living, with his stinking pet hare, spending the best part of his pension on beer and tobacco. Every winter she expected the treacherous, icy roads to bring him low. He was a big man and heavy, one good fall might finish him off. When he was gone, it would be good riddance to bad rubbish. Night after night he came and drank his four half-pints in the Greyhound bar, but in all the years he never once bought her so much as a mouthful of ale. Unforgiving old devil, that's what he was. She would do a jig on his grave if it cracked her ankle, she would that.

Yes, there would be things done the night on which Asa died as would be the talk of Grovelace long after his body became rotten. For supper, she and Clara would eat the tame hare; she would get drunk to celebrate. A tear slid down her face as she raged against the old man she had chosen so many years before. How could a woman have known? Yet if she had taken the stableman he might have turned out like the Greyhound landlord.

That Ivy; there was plenty to do with a husband like that. No wonder she had not spotted Clara's game yet.

In spite of his tricks and all, landlord was a nice man. A drink could be coaxed from him as easy as easy. It would be an unkind day to all the Grovelace loungers when Mr. Flack quitted the place. Townspeople knew too much or thought they did, but those as came Grovelace way learnt a few hard facts.

The Greyhound kitchen was full of relics. Incoming people brought this thing, outgoing folk left that. Mrs. Tapin knew everything in the room, and its history. Skelts left behind the shining Welsh dresser with its lustre jugs and blue china. They were a poor lot, that family. Mrs. Tapin did not think they could ever have come by the dresser honest, in the first place. The dresser she would like. The day the Flacks moved in she came up with offers of help; anxious to see what the new tenants brought in the way of furniture and household goods. She was very impressed by Mrs. Flack's heavy bedroom suite. Best of all, they set Clara on as barmaid without any trouble whatever. Mrs. Tapin was promised two or three days' charing each week. The new people pleased her very well. They were slipshod, easy to cheat, barring young Tom. Mrs. Tapin sniffed. If ever she could do that young man an ill turn she would, with great pleasure. She tried to set George Phips on to him. George was sweet on Clara, but he was as obstinate as a lame duck. "Nought wrong with Tom, as I see," he told her; "he don't muck Clara about." He did not. It was his attitude to Clara that gave Mrs. Tapin most offence. Mrs. Tapin thought he ought to make up to the girl. Treat her flirty like. Instead of that he was like a blind man, and never gave Clara a sly look even. A bit different from the landlord. Fred Flack saw all the girl's good points very quick. He was a gay dog. A bit too gay, Clara would find, if she was not careful.

Mrs. Tapin stirred up the fire, setting the kettle down on the glowing red coals. She would be glad of a nice swill of tea herself. The kettle soon started to sing; she got the teapot down and set it to warm on the hob.

Grovelace was a nice place. She knew of none better. Of the three clustering villages, Grovelace was the smallest. Scrutton might possess a mine and Straycross shops, but Grovelace owned a Hall and a Squire; of both they were proud. They laughed at Straycross and its inhabitants. Everyone knew Straycross was at the world's end. A long road wound from Grovelace through Straycross in a loop back to its starting-place. Whichever way Straycross folks went they had to pass through Grovelace. It was a fine joke, that. It narked Straycross folk nicely.

Scrutton was a mining village, dirty and small.

Though but a hamlet of forty cottages and a public-house, Grovelace regarded itself as the most important of the three places. If anyone argued, they held up the Hall and Squire Grovedon. That was enough. He owned Scrutton mine and Straycross village. Almost owned the people, for from his land, his property, they gained a hard livelihood. The Hall on Grovelace Hill overlooked them all.

Times were hard. The war, which put pianos into their homes, had depleted the ranks of their young, vigorous, wage-earning men. The cottages swarmed with wild children. Girls, when they left Straycross School, got a job in the shoe factory, or went away to service in one of the big northern towns. Often they would never come back to Grovelace. The village did not make strangers welcome. Those who went wrong were wise to stay away.

The villagers did not like to see strangers in the Greyhound, but the choice did not lie with them. During the war the old Squire disposed of the inn to a wealthy Staffordshire brewery company. Not even the Grovedons had a say in the matter nowadays.

Mrs. Tapin sighed.

Times were indeed changed. She made the tea and left it to draw. In a few moments she poured out four cupfuls, her own last. Mr. Flack would not need a cup. She took a long drink from her own cup; putting the others on a tray, she carried them upstairs.

II

DARKNESS crept up over the hill, and the rain fell with dull, heavy persistence. Leaning with his arms on the window-ledge, Tom Oakley watched with increasing misery. The darkening hillside fields were sodden, the naked trees shivered and dripped.

Business would be poor that night, Tom knew. The miners who sometimes walked over from Scrutton would stay in the warm tap-room of the Black Horse. It might pour with rain any night but Friday, Saturday and Sunday without affecting the Greyhound's trade. Tom felt Nature was against them too. If they could only hold on till August, summer might recoup winter's loss. Char-à-banc parties streaming from the towns would bring a golden harvest to the Greyhound. Tom pictured swirling crowds of men from Nottingham, Sheffield, and other towns filling the house to overflowing, spending money lavishly. He knew it for an idle dream. When summer came, God alone knew where they would be. Of one thing he felt certain, they would be out of the Greyhound. It had been a mistake ever to come. A grave mistake. He thought of the false promise of the first night. Then the Greyhound had overflowed with prospective customers, drinking and cheerful. In the passage, in the kitchen even, they stood. He, Ivy and Freddy worked like slaves, serving free first drinks to every person. For miles around the villagers came to drink with them; to wish them prosperity and health. Neither Tom nor Ivy with all their experience understood the bleak significance of this. They did not know the simple pleasures of country-folk, who thoroughly enjoy a walk of seven miles if a free half-pint of good ale awaits them. The ignorant Freddy was wildly excited. Only with difficulty they persuaded him not to make open house that night. The pleasant deference went to his head; he forgot that it cost nothing. Tom sighed. That had been a good night at the Greyhound; until they left he would not see such another.

He thought regretfully of the old days when his father kept the Crown and Cushion in Birmingham. Good old Brum, there was no other place quite like it. Those were the days: from the Bull Ring came a steady flow of custom during the house's open hours. Market-men, porters from the Midland Station, and the street hawkers used the place regularly, and there had always been a good number of chance people.

His father, old Tom, was well known and respected for an upright man. In Brum there had been no need to evade the regulation hours, trade was so good and steady. The police never worried old Tom; they spoke well of the Crown. That was how a licensed house should be conducted, they said. The even tenor of the old man's control never altered, no matter what the day—"Business as usual" had been his motto.

On Saturday nights, market days and bank holidays he patrolled the house like a policeman. His steady efforts caused his regular customers to take almost as much pride in the Crown's reputation as he did himself. Fat Mrs. Oakley held the same degree of popularity with her customers and she brought up her two children to deserve the deference they received. Mrs. Oakley was born in the trade herself, so she knew the kind of adulation publicans' children received. Part of it was reflected glory, for poor townspeople consider the landlord of a public-house to be a successful man. The other part came from a customer's desire to be well in with her and the children's father. From Mrs. Oakley's training Tom and Ivy grew up pleasant and considerate. Toy hawkers in the Bull Ring gutter talked admiringly of the Oakley children's behaviour. They were chips of the old block. Good old Tom. Good old Esther. Childhood gone by, then, the Oakley children really took their share in the Crown's trade. In the morning Ivy did kitchen work, at night she went behind the serving bar in the smoke-room. Young Tom learnt everything from the cellar work to marking in the billiard-room. Nothing could be shirked, not even the hateful job of cleaning beer pumps at eleven o'clock every Friday night. When he got used to the work, he was all right. He loved the life and knew it from A to Z.

To gain wider experience his father made him work for eighteen months at the Old Waterloo Bar. Ivy, too, possessed equal knowledge and skill; she could tap a barrel or tilt a cask neatly. Work in a public-house has short hours of frantic serving, a few hours' real hard labour in the cellars and yards; the other easy times are the publican's reward. Tom always liked the life; he knew no other ambition than to be landlord of an hotel himself some day. The respectful esteem in which his father was held seemed to Tom a high enough thing to aim for. In those days at Birmingham life was very different. Old Tom spent money without stint; if his wife and daughter wanted a thing they had it. Both Ivy and Tom received twenty-five shillings a week as wages. Tom was fond of clothes; he owned plenty, also shoes with narrow, pointed toes. There was always something doing in Brum. He and Ivy got a regular half-day out once a week. Sometimes he went to the Alex. Theatre, or to a show at one of the music halls. If Ivy was free the same night, they went off to the Palais de Danse together. Tom had been very good on his feet; the "Pros" danced with him free if not too busy with rich patrons. Sometimes they went on to a late dance after closing time at the Crown. For the Police Ball and the Licensed Victuallers', the whole family turned out, but those affairs were so crowded, folks could only just surge round the dance floor. There they met, drank and danced with old trade friends whom they seldom saw at other times. Such dances were very jolly. Everyone came determined to enjoy themselves, and the charity for which the dance was organised benefited accordingly. The Oakleys turned up dressed in their most magnificent clothes. Esther and Ivy went to London a week before to buy gowns. Mrs. Oakley's taste was for something gay, and at the ball if people saw a large woman in a very bright gown they would know she had arrived.

Ivy could wear anything. Though not beautiful she had an air of smartness that most of the men found attractive. It was at a Police Ball she met Freddy Flack. Like most publican's daughters, she had acquired the knack of keeping men at a friendly distance. All the Crown customers had known just how far Ivy would allow them to go. Whenever a too conceited youngster overstepped the mark Ivy slapped his face hard. But over Freddy she lost her heart and head. He was everything a woman could desire, she felt. That he was in love with her, she found almost too wonderful to be true. Their courtship lasted one glorious year. Ivy wanted to be married. The queer stories of Freddy's past she could not listen to, though both the Oakley men had heard plenty about him. The wedding took place in great style. Ivy had five bridesmaids and a train.

In spite of his dislike for Freddy, whom he did not trust, Tom was best man. There were more than a hundred wedding presents. The patrons of the Crown gave Ivy a china tea service. Tom would never forget that day. Everyone they knew came to the church. For Tom, when Ivy left on her honeymoon, the gay party fell flat. The coarse allusions made by some of the hilarious guests hurt him; it was unbelievable that they could hint of such things about Ivy. His hatred and jealousy of Fred grew steadily from that night. The thought of the young couple being all in all to each other made him bitter. Since the beginning of memory he loved Ivy, worshipped her. No matter what fault others found in her, always he had sought to shield and defend her from them. That love had been the one thing in his life. Ivy returned it till Freddy Flack came on the scene, then she was hurt at Tom's lack of kind feeling towards the man she had chosen. When she was gone, life became dull for Tom at the Crown. He thought seriously of getting work in a London hotel. Things between him and Ivy could never be the same again. Never. The thought saddened him, increased his feeling of dislike towards Fred.

There were eight or nine other young fellows Ivy might have married, all more suitable in Tom's opinion than the one she chose. Arthur Wilkins had been devoted to her. Of him Tom fully approved. He was a steady, hard-working chap, the son of a publican. Ivy and he could have taken their pick of the Wooten brewery houses. Poor Arthur, Ivy might have taken him eventually if Flack had not turned up. But lacking Flack's physique and ardour, the older man dropped straight out of Ivy's reckoning.

Two years later the landlord of the Crown and his wife were dead. After thirty-five years of married happiness, they died within an hour of each other, having eaten something that poisoned them. After lying ill for two days, Esther had gone. Old Tom seemed to be rallying, when suddenly he closed his eyes and never opened them on life again. The news stunned Ivy. For a few days Tom had her to himself. She did not seem as though she could bear contact with anyone else. After the grand funeral the will was read. In the event of his wife dying first, old Tom bequeathed his money to the two children. They were to have equal shares. So Ivy went back to her husband with two hundred and fifty pounds. Tom banked his money and got a job in London. While in London he and Ivy corresponded every week. Ivy's letters were bald and bright. They did nothing to make him believe in her happiness. Freddy was a bit too fond of drink, though Ivy seldom wrote anything. Tom decided that drink was the trouble. He and Ivy were too carefully trained ever to let such a habit grow on themselves. From business acuteness they never refused to drink with a customer, but while beer was paid for, all they consumed was cold tea from a hidden jug. Even old Tom, who held teetotallers in utter contempt, had kept a gin-labelled bottle full of cold water, from which he and Esther might drink, as he termed it, "the one over the eight." Tom never drank liquor in business hours, though the temptation was strong at times. Life in London was lonely. Women had no attraction for him. Men respected rather than liked him. He worked hard, saving most of the money he earned. Once a month he went up to the West End for a lonely treat: some extravagance that vainly recalled the old joys of an evening's razzle with Ivy. But the old spirit had gone; the taste for music halls was dead, now Ivy was not there to hear of what he had seen and heard.

After a few months in an Aldgate public-house, he felt a change would be pleasant. To gain wider experience he applied for work at a smart hotel registry office in Hart Street. The manageress liked him; she thought his quiet manner would help him to make a successful waiter at one of the very exclusive hotels. She was proud of her own capacity for attracting an excellent class of hotel servants to her office. All the best hotels put their names down on her books. Through her services, Tom found work at the Bristol Hotel. The work suited him. In laying a table or serving a meal, he worked with deft quietness. The work was a source of increasing pleasure to him; he found the severe, unchangeable mode of serving a meal correctly had a quality of satisfaction about it. After two days, the housekeeper, who trained him, considered him ready to be given a floor station. Like all other beginners he started on the third floor. Tom grew increasingly happy in his new work. He wrote to Ivy long, enthusiastic letters about it. When he had been at the Bristol six months, he received a letter from Ivy; she was very excited, almost incoherent. From it, Tom gathered she and Freddy were taking a little public-house up in North Derbyshire. She implored him to join them. During his hours of ease, Tom sat in the service-room staring at her letter. He read it a dozen times or more.

From his first reading he knew he would go. To leave the Bristol, where he was happy and comfortable, would be a wrench. But really if Ivy wanted him, what did that matter? When the relieving waiter came on duty, Tom went down to the staff office and gave the manager his notice. No one else at the Bristol knew he was leaving; his last day there passed quietly. The manager brought up his pay slip, and told him: "If you ever want to come back to us, Oakley, send me a letter. You are a good lad, and I am sorry to lose you." Tom thanked him. Next day he left St. Pancras Station *en route* for Chesterfield. The whole thing possessed the unreality of a dream. He stared at the other people in the carriage, two serious women and an elderly man. From the scraps of conversation that drifted his way, he knew they were rushing to the bedside of a dying friend. The youngest woman kept saying frantically, "I shall never forgive myself if we are too late." The others tried to comfort her, but she had become obsessed by remorse. Each time the train roared through a town or village, the old man named it with an air of proud accomplishment. Every thump of the wheels hurried them a second nearer the desire of their hearts. Tom's happiness grew so that his heart swelled with loving kindness towards anyone and everyone; even Freddy should be liked and admired. He wished to tell these poor, desperate passengers, "Your friend is well. Out of danger, of that I am certain." Once or twice his licked his lips, turning towards them to speak. But their grief built them a wall. They did not think of him at all, not looking his way. After a little stay at Leicester, the train fled on. She seemed to attain terrific speed, and triumphant wheels told Tom, nearer, nearer, nearer, nearer. At Derby he would have to change; Ivy and Freddy would be waiting to meet him. The thought of Ivy was sheer delight; but for the other desperate people he would have hummed a gay tune, dancing his feet on the carriage floor. In all the wide world there was no other as Ivy was, no one. When she was happy, her every gesture gave him joy; if she was sad, her sorrow wounded his heart. From all that was ugly, from all bitterness he wished to shield her. The feelings he had for her were too ecstatic to set in a frame of words. The train darted through a tiny grass-banked station. "Spondon!" gasped the old man thankfully; "Derby in a moment now." Then came the business of collecting suit-cases and coats. Tom sat, waiting till the others left the carriage; he was bursting with impatience; he lugged his two heavy suit-cases through the awkward door. Derby at last. The station was huge and cold; it lacked Birmingham's friendly untidiness and bustle. Staggering towards the huge clock he passed his travelling companions. A young man was with them, and from their huddled misery he knew they had arrived too late. Something at his heart tugged; he felt a little sick. Ivy rushed towards him, on her head a little scarlet toque. He dropped the cases, and she took him in her arms, crying and laughing, such joy was theirs. Freddy hurried up, smiling and jovial. Tom noticed he was a little redder in the face. Just to look at Ivy and press her hands, to catch her eye and smile, was Tom's delight. Both she and her husband were in high spirits. They knew Tom would like the pub; it was a jolly little place, and, of course, they would only be there for a year, after that they would get a town house—somewhere. In these days everyone wanted publics; they were hard to get. The valuations had increased too; that made them decide on the Greyhound—they could start there free from debt. Tom should hear all about everything. Most of the furniture Ivy acquired on marriage had been sold, but the things belonging to their mother she kept; they should furnish the sitting and guest rooms. That gave Tom a happy feeling. It would be nice living among the old familiar things of his childhood and youth. After a light lunch at the station buffet, they took the slow local train to Chesterfield. Brother and sister sat side by side. Ivy's closeness was sweet, Tom felt; he kept touching her arm gently, with stroking fingers. His love for her swelled, embracing Fred. Because of her, Fred should find in him a brother.

They talked of old times at the Crown. The prospects of being back in the trade thrilled Ivy. She had rosy dreams of a return to Birmingham, and a public-house there, in a future made near by confidence and hope. Both she and Fred looked well; they teased Tom a little on account of his pallor. The Flacks were lodging in Chesterfield for the night. Tom stayed at the same house. Excitement made them all restless, Freddy most of all. When tea was over, Freddy suggested that Tom should go out with him for a drink. He did not want to, but in his desire to please Freddy, he hedged. Presently Ivy, seeing her husband's impatience, said, "You go alone, dear. Tom and me have such a lot to talk over." Both men were pleased; neither really wished for the other's companionship, yet both acted from an impulse of friendliness. When her husband was gone, Ivy's brother learnt the whole history of the Greyhound affair. After the Oakleys left the Crown, Ivy ceased going out with Freddy every evening; her only reason for going to the Crown was to see her own people, and to give a hand when they were very busy. So Fred had found another pub very differently run from the Crown. The landlord was not much class; he sold stuff after hours. And his house was frequented by betting touts. Tom knew the kind of place.

Fred was too generous by nature. People cheated him right and left. If only Ivy had known in time the kind of gang he was getting in with, she felt that he might have been got away from them. But she hadn't. Things started to go wrong. Fred lost job after job. He would let any business slide to attend a race meeting. Of course, employers were not going to stand that, and his occasional lucky wins helped on his dislike of ordinary work. One night he came home and told Ivy he had chucked his job at the garage, having been there less than a month. She rowed at him tearfully, but he told her confidently he had found better work. Dick Mull, the bookmaker, wanted him as a general help. Life had taught Ivy something of that sort of job; she knew it was little better than that of an ordinary street-corner tout. It was useless to argue with Freddy; after reviling her in rage, he would weep, swearing to make good. Next morning Ivy saw the garage proprietor. As she thought, it was he who sacked Freddy, not Freddy him. She did not say anything to her husband; it was useless to begin another row, even more futile than the last. So Freddy started his new job. For a short while things went well, then luck started to be uncertain. Horses were queer, uncertain creatures.

One week he would earn good commission, and bet fortunately. When things were good like that they lived on the fat of the land, feeding at hotels and buying clothes. Ivy admitted that such times were fine; she had enjoyed them thoroughly. Suddenly things would go wrong, Freddy could neither collect bets, nor discover winners; often he would turn up on Saturday night without a copper. He spent more and more on drink: clients expected him to drink with them if their luck was in, and to drink with him if it was out. Freddy grew steadily more fond of intoxicants; he would swallow a single neat whisky at one gulp. Sometimes Ivy was obliged to pawn clothes for food and rent, and once the bailiffs were actually in possession. That frightened her badly. Freddy had a very fortunate and timely win, the bill was paid, and Ivy's furniture was her own again. After that she nagged at him, hard and often, but he won by saying, "Next time the bums come in, my dear, if you want to keep your blasted furniture you'll have to go to the bank and tap your fortune." She knew he meant what he said. Two hundred and fifty pounds would soon be swallowed up in paying debts that he incurred. She was frightened; she did not know where Fred would stop.

Having no legal knowledge, she had no idea of the law's powers. The first time her furniture was nearly taken; they might try for it again. To cap everything, a woman friend came in one night and warned her

Fred was known to the police; it was merely a matter of time before they caught him in the act. Of the truth of this information Ivy knew. Her friend was the sister of a police constable. But while to herself the warning served, Freddy obstinately refused to take any notice of it. The police would never get him, he was far too smart. Besides, he knew them all, and except for an odd one or two, they were all darn good fellows. Ivy smiled: he was like a young boy. He knew everything, and no one could tell him anything. Having failed with her husband, Ivy waited till the public-houses were open next morning, then she went round to the bookmaker's office and saw Dick Mull. He listened to her tale keenly, then asked, "What do you want me to do, eh?" Ivy answered, "Give him the sack; he won't be much use to you if there's a conviction against him." Dick thought it out: he had not much use for men known to the police; Freddy was not so good as he had been at first. Once the police caught him, his clients would get the wind up, and their money would go to some other tout. He promised to think it over.

As soon as she saw Freddy's face, Ivy knew that something had gone wrong. Her heart thudded, she felt excited. At last Freddy blurted his troubles out. He had been working his usual round all day, without collecting scarcely a bet. When he got back to the office with the slips Dick said disgustedly, "You quit, son, and take up bus conducting." Turning her face away, Ivy smiled. "It was so funny," she told Tom gaily; "Freddy was that upset, he nearly cried. He got another job back in a garage."

Then Ivy set to work quietly to find out all she could about a public-house licence. At last she knew all the necessary things, and decided that she and Fred could take one with her money. The sum was too small to get any but the meanest of out-of-the-way houses in Birmingham. Also, Ivy knew what it would be if they got a house anywhere in the town; all Freddy's sporting friends would come. The house would soon get a bad name. Later, when Freddy learnt the trade, it would be different. He would soon learn how things were done. When Ivy told Fred what she wished to do, he was delighted. They talked over the coming venture for hours at a time, Freddy promised a complete reformation. She had had misgivings at times, but Freddy did seem as though he was really going to steady down into a quiet, sober and prosperous landlord of a country inn. The only real trouble was over Tom. Freddy did not want him, and Ivy did. She won, being in control of the situation by reason of her money. When she knew that the boy would join them, she was overjoyed, she told Freddy quietly; he only smiled dully and said, "Well, I'm glad for your sake."

Ivy's tale ended, she began to worry. Fred ought to be back by now; they needed a good long night's sleep. It was just like him to go and do something silly. That was the kind of trick Fred played. No one ever knew what he would do. She and Tom set out in search of him but in all the public-houses they visited, he was not to be found. Ivy was upset and ready to cry. Her superstitious nature saw a bad omen in Freddy's slip. At eleven he came back, not drunk, though his voice was thick. In her rage Ivy flared out, denouncing him. A grave look came over Tom's face. He hated trouble of that kind; no good ever came of it. Poor Ivy, from her bald story, her life as a married woman was not very easy. Ivy kept on complaining; she took no notice of the humble look in Fred's eyes. At last it changed, becoming venomous. The violence of the ensuing quarrel shook Tom; he listened to the wrongs which each accused the other of committing. Both made points; they reviled each other with such contempt that for them to love each other seemed impossible.

Such thoughts saddened Tom, stripped life of joy. For Ivy's sake he must be more bright, make more effort to get on with Freddy. Keep on trying, though goodness knew what the future held.

Tom lifted his head from the nest of his arm; it was quite dark. He felt as though he had just awakened from sleep, but of that he was not sure. When the lamp was lit, he drew the curtains. The shadows jumped startlingly on the walls; the one he cast looked huge and menacing. Would Ivy and Fred stand any chance of happiness and success if he cleared out? Tom considered this question soberly, trying to detach his own personality from it. For a time Fred might reform to celebrate his victory. What about Ivy? She would break up soon; with drink there waiting to comfort her, she would take it, take it gratefully. If only that was the end of Ivy's trouble: to become a drunkard. To Tom's brain, seared by the cruelty Ivy endured, her whole existence seemed anguished. Why did he have to stand by and see her suffer? Fred's childish unconcern for her. . . . That was what was wrong with Freddy; he was childlike, a small boy who played with one thing and destroyed another. His affection and hatreds were the same, too.

Tom looked out his clothes, ready for the evening. When they were ready, he stripped, washing himself a limb at a time. The cold water made him shudder, but he kept on till satisfied of his body's refreshment. Freddy was a stupid fool. Everything lay to his fingers for success to come. He had so much Tom desired. The boy thought wistfully of Freddy's possessions, things in which one should take pride. Rubbing down his body, Tom thought of Freddy's, which was fine and strong. If he worked hard, the fine things could be kept; of that Tom felt sure, though he knew that soon any such effort would be too late. Mrs. Tapin, Clara and himself ought to go. The Greyhound could support two economical workers, but not five. He could talk things over, first with Ivy, then with Fred—give them his suggestions, do all he could to help them jointly; that would be the best help for Ivy in the long run. She, he knew, would work hard enough if only Fred gave signs of helping her. The two of them could not fall to utter ruin in front of his watching eyes; it was incredible. It was a pity that he and Fred did not get on better together, but to hear Ivy speak her husband's name was enough to upset him. With him out of the way they might do better. A knock came on the door. Tom sat down on the bed, throwing a blanket over his lower half. Mrs. Tapin's head appeared round the door, then her hand offering him a cup of tea.

III

IT was quite dark. Vaguely Ivy was conscious that Mrs. Tapin brought her a cup of tea, but she enjoyed lying still in the warm bed. She would like to lie there for ever, with Freddy at her side, near enough for her to touch. That was silly. She must get up. She reached blindly for her watch; its luminous dial told her she could stay in bed for a further twenty minutes. The tea was tepid when she sat up to drink it; a little slopped over the cup rim on to her night-gown.

Now she was awake and conscious of her troubles. The chief of them was Freddy. In spite of all Tom said, he was a good lad, a bit wild and foolish perhaps. If only he would leave the house to Tom and herself, everything would come all right. She and Tom knew the trade inside out. In summer-time there would be catering to do for exploring motorists. Food was more profitable than drink. A shilling for a ham sandwich. She could make eightpence profit on that at least. The ham carved thin as paper, as she knew how to cut it. Then there would be workmen's outings from the towns. Eighteenpence for a fancy tea, a shilling for a plain one, that's how they would make money. In the autumn they could leave the Greyhound and get a new public-house in one of the Midland towns. Near enough to Birmingham for her and Tom to go at times. Wolverhampton, she heard, was a good place. Freddy could get a job; she and Tom would look after the House. There was not enough for Fred to do to keep him out of harm here. Tom knew the trade, Freddy never would. He was too generous and impulsive. People who kept public-houses were not expected to be generous; only on very rare occasions were they expected to stand drinks. Tom knew just when to; every person who spoke to Freddy amiably he wanted to stand them a drink. It was not out of his own pocket, either, but out of the till. That kind of thing was damn foolishness. Young Clara was getting too fresh with Freddy. He was a fool with women. It would be the girl's fault for tempting him on. The first time she caught them Clara would go. Mrs. Tapin ought to speak to Clara.

Ivy wondered if she had had a child would Freddy have kept faithful to her. She decided he would not. He was too easy a prey for any attractive woman. That other women wanted Freddy, she found pleasing, but his taking them she hated. Freddy! women! women had done their utmost to spoil him, she too. It was hard to refuse him anything, almost impossible. If blustering did not succeed, he could cry like a frightened child, his head on her breast. Then she was his mother, he her son, and the victory in his grasp. Victory gave him back his manhood; in a moment he was fiercely possessive man and she his woman. At times for his foolish pigheaded obstinacy she could have killed him. When he was drunk, the maudlin expressions of his affection nauseated her, but when he wept she was conquered. Youth, charm and beauty he had; for those things alone he could keep her love.

Freddy was without morals. None of the virtues appealed to him. He was utterly incapable of assuming responsibility, yet insisted that all such things were under his sole guidance. It pleased him to play at being landlord; the easy popularity he obtained by giving away free beer pleased him immensely. He drank far too much, a bad thing for any publican; he was extravagant. The greyhound, Pertinax, he paid five pounds for—a young whippet bought at Chesterfield market for ten-and-six would have done more to earn its keep. Ivy felt a moment's panic: the way Freddy was spending money would ruin them. Only that day, at lunch-time, a miner came in and tried to collect two pounds which he declared Fred owed him over a game of banker. The money wouldn't last for ever. He owed the brewers money, she knew. They were safeguarded; she had paid them two hundred and fifty pounds, their valuation of the Greyhound's inventory. Why wouldn't he let her know how much he was in debt to them? Tom wanted her to leave him; at times she wished that she could. If only he loved her as she loved him, things would be so different. There was no one else like Freddy in the world, with all his faults. For better or worse she had taken him; whatever happened she would stay by him. Bad luck would not always follow them. It was sure to change sooner or later.

She must talk things over with Tom. Try and cheer him up, make him see the bright side of things; bless him, he was a good lad. No girl ever had a better brother, though he was a bit gloomy at times. Silly old Tom, he never did like Freddy much; it was funny that he should be so jealous. They would not have stayed a month at the Greyhound without him; she could not have run the place by herself, and Freddy was nearly useless.

Perhaps it had been a mistake to take a pub, as Tom thought. But then Freddy was out of work, and his friends led him into bad ways. He promised faithfully only to drink what customers stood him. The first day saw that promise broken; still she had hoped when the first excitement settled down he would settle too. But he did not. He could not do without men friends, and he never made one that was any use to him. Night after night the sporting men came over from Scrutton to fleece him, and drink his treats. He thought himself clever, but they knew him for a mug. Ivy was sure they cheated at cards. One of them sold him Pertinax; the dog was no good, it always ran last on the course, yet Freddy still trusted the man who sold him the dog. Trust a man till you catch him out once, was fair enough. She had never been able to trust Freddy after she caught him with the chambermaid at the hotel where they stayed on their wedding night. She had seen the woman in his arms. It had been terrible, yet she forgave him, perhaps too quickly. Saturday night at the Greyhound was hateful; before the bar opened she felt blue. Freddy always drank too much; the excitement of a full house went to his head. He was such a boy.

When summer came she would feel better. Winter, the sad, bleak season when even the earth was weary, the trees bare and the sad fields frost-ravaged, made her sad. At moments life seemed a dull futility, and her mind ached from thought. When hunger-brave birds came to her door, driven by cold, she fed them, wondering at their desire to live.

Ivy did not like the Derbyshire folks who were her customers; they had some virtues, but their vices seemed many. They were slow to like strangers, though quick enough to hate. She knew how to treat them in their own coin, with contempt and haughtiness. They despised Freddy; that was natural enough. With all her love of him, she knew his faults, knew them only too well—his laziness and boasting which the country-folk so despised. He thought country people fools. They were a damn sight too smart for him, tricking him skilfully. People who earned every penny hard, ripping it from the grudging earth, were not fools. They earned hard and kept hard. They cheated, as Freddy tried to. Ivy held them in respect, in spite of her dislike. She could always tell when there had been some crooked game going on. At those times money was spent more freely.

She never dreamed that life could be so hard as it proved to be in Grovelace village. Every penny they could scrape ought to be saved towards a move for the better. If only she could make Freddy see how wise and reasonable that was, they might look forward to prosperity in some town public-house. In towns people spent money freely; they drew winnings over horse-racing and sweepstakes. Townspeople were kinder, less thrifty than country-folk. If only she'd known, she would have stayed in Birmingham, even though Freddy had had no regular work. Quite easily she could have got an excellent job as a barmaid which would have kept them going. It was too late now: all her eggs were in one basket, and that not in her own keeping. Still, she must struggle on trying not to be hard on Fred, poor boy; he was his own worst enemy. If only he could know that, if only she could make him see it, there was nothing she would not do. She thought of Fred in her mind, forcing him onward with an intensity that was almost physical. With strength of mind and a will to success, those things his, and on his shoulders they would all come through. If only he would try. Whatever he did, she would always love him; it was impossible to be indifferent to him. In the early days his coming swept her straight off her feet. The calm, possessive way in which he danced with her so that no other man ventured near her except Tom. From that first night she was his; she had thought of him hourly, spinning herself a shining dream of life ahead with him. Those days were the best of all. She had known the sound that his foot made on the step. Every evening when she heard, her heart leapt. To have him touch her, to touch him, mazed her brain; she served her other customers dimly. They receded from her consciousness like dreams. Those were the days, the best of her life. Yet now so distant, their reality seemed dream-like. Her love struggled on. Sometimes she knew Freddy loved her, at other times she doubted him. He took life so lightly in the main. Yet if she worried or complained, it upset him at once. She was aggrieved by his failure to take up the responsibility of his married state, and in the management of the house. It was a blow to her pride in him. Things were difficult; if he did do anything of importance, she needed to watch him because he was likely to make foolish mistakes.

Always she hoped to see a subtle change take place in his nature. Hope and dreams kept her from despair. One day Fred would alter. He was young in mind and experience, a boy.

Ivy got out of bed and lit the lamp. She drew the window curtains, then sat down in front of the dressing-table to brush her hair. The glass showed tiny lines at her eyes and mouth. She looked thirty, these days. Freddy was two years younger and Tom six years. When Tom was a little boy she had been like a mother to him. That perhaps accounted for the way he loved her. Of his devotion she was so certain that she scarcely ever thought about it. Curious that was. Would she have received Freddy's complete devotion in the same careless manner? She did not think so. Life would be too full of rapture. In the first happy months of their courting, she never needed Tom. Now she did need him badly. Life at the Greyhound without him would not be bearable. He was the only steady person on whom she could rely. He worked hard, early and late; there was no job too unpleasant for him to tackle. That was how Fred should be. Careful, willing and keen, ready for stray opportunity. Tom was almost perfect for a publican's job. People respected him, they knew he would be hard to deceive; not many tried tricks on him.

Ivy could never dissociate what was from what she hoped would be. The two things blended in her thoughts, unbalancing her judgment.

Time had fled by bringing no improvement in her husband's character. Yet she always felt another day would produce the desired qualities in him. Hope was so vivid in her thoughts that she found it incredible to believe that Freddy remained the same easy-going man.

She lacked honesty of mind where he was concerned. The truth about him was too unpleasant to believe; she only accepted the obvious faults which could not be disregarded. He had many good points; she dwelt on them pleasantly. The beauty of his straight limbs, his strength, the whiteness of his body, the tender, secret things of which she alone knew. He was generous to a fault, happy in disposition, good to look at. She liked to watch him set out for a day's sport, Naxi at his heels; they made a handsome pair, master and dog, even though the bag they brought home was a poor one. Fred was a fine man; no one, not even Tom, could deny that —six foot tall, broad and muscular, his hair the colour of ripe sunlit corn, his eyes blue like flowers.

Few women had such a mate, Ivy knew. For a time they must let him play, childlike, at being landlord. When he tired, she and Tom would make things pay.

Certainly he was a problem. Her suspicions of his interest in Clara became more definite. Why, she could not think. Perhaps it was in the way Fred spoke to the girl these days, as though there was an understanding between them.

Tom suspected something too. "You keep an eye on that girl," he warned her; "she is getting too keen on your old man." He had told her that weeks ago now.

Perhaps she was too late already. For the future she would keep a close watch.

Ivy dressed, putting on a black skirt and jumper. Business came slowly at first. When the night drew on, people drank more, as though to make up for time lost. Tom would be down ready before six; he always was—she could depend on that.

One of her customers was getting too fresh, Josh Brightman. When she told Freddy he only laughed. Tom had better know. He would treat her complaint seriously; it was no laughing matter. Tom would advise her what to do. Slapping Brightman across the face did not stop his tricks; it made the tap-room roar with laughter, and herself humiliated, ashamed. After all, she would not tell Tom! Giving herself a last look in the glass, she went along to the guest-room where Freddy rested. She opened the door softly. He was fast asleep. A letter lay fallen from his pocket by the bedside. Picking it up, she recognised Clara's handwriting on the unopened envelope. Pinching the light from her candle, she crept from the room. Locked in her sitting-room, she lit the lamp, then examined the envelope carefully. It was made of cheap paper, poorly gummed; it opened quickly without tearing. She read the note.

"DEAR FRED,
"Am seeing B. G. to-night. Will tell you all news later. A. T.
"CLARA."

There was not much in that. Still, why had Clara written at all? And what did A. T. mean?

She stuck the envelope down. Going back to Fred's room in the dark, she dropped the letter by his bed. He slept on heavily.

Ivy sighed and went slowly down the stairs.

IV

ON either side of the battered mirror a candle burnt. Anxiously Clara gazed at her uncertain reflection. The mirror was old and the light bad; surely she could not look so ghastly as the mirror made out. She was cheered by the thought. Her mother would have said something—not much missed her, Clara knew well.

Going to the cupboard, she took out the jumper Fred gave her for Christmas; she had done well out of him. He was better than the dull Grovelace boys who never bought her anything if they could help it. Not that she let them do what Fred had done. She had not meant him to, either, only he was too quick for her, a type fresh to her experience.

Clara returned to thoughts of a long-nurtured ambition. She wanted to get away from Grovelace, away from the dull, thrifty men and the spiteful women. Away from her too sharp mother, and from her beastly foster-father. Once away she would never return. The unknown life in towns played on her imagination. No matter what the cost she would go. If only Fred would run away with her, away from his soppy wife and bad-tempered brother-in-law. Clara liked Fred, but she knew he would be no use to her in the long run. Even if Ivy divorced him, she had no intention of marrying him. Unlike Ivy, she saw that Fred only loved himself; that was how she felt about herself too. When Fred had served her purpose he might go to the devil. Clara possessed all the beauty of the Grovedon women, their delicate fairness of skin. Often when the Squire was away she would persuade old Blakin to let her see the family portraits. It thrilled her to see them, for there she saw herself. She possessed their tallness, their proud bearing, her hair was straight and gold like theirs, her eye the same hard blue. Her dead father's portrait hung there too. Clara gazed on it with fierce hatred; she was proud of the blood he had given her, but for the common woman he had made her mother she loathed him. The dreams she had had of being a legitimate Grovedon were puffed-up emptiness. If the Grovedons met her in the village they gave her the curt greeting they reserved for common folk. Yet the vain dreams often came. She behaved in a manner she considered ladylike, but such refinements were only the surface. Her mind held the same coarse images that her mother saw. Every man Clara met she considered in the light of a victim, possible or impossible. On both kinds she tried her skill. Some were too easy. It amused Clara to excite them; it gave her a sense of power. When she had led a man on to a pitch of desire, she turned on him with cold bitterness, destroying the illusion he had built up around her. Such games were all that made existence in Grovelace bearable. On her day out she went to Chesterfield by bus from Scrutton village. She found the small town dull enough, but she liked to have strange men stare after her in the street. If one spoke to her, she considered him quickly; if his clothes and speech were decent, she would agree to walk with him. The thing then was to make him spend money. If he proved what she scornfully called "the walking sort," she soon got rid of him. The day was too short and the time too precious to waste on unprofitable dallying.

One day strolling through the busy market-place, she saw Fred a few paces ahead. She overtook him and he spoke to her. The rest was simple. After a meal they went to the pictures. Clara was delighted at her success.

From the first she had considered Fred as a possible admirer, but the ease with which she got him was amazing. At that time she did not know Fred. He, having wandered alone round Chesterfield all morning, was feeling bored and miserable. The sight of Clara did him good.

Her bright hardness amused him, her beauty of form and, most of all, her youth attracted him. The fact of her being a barmaid at the Greyhound lent an added thrill to the affair for him. Brought up, or as Ivy told him dragged up, without respect for women, Fred wasted little time on the diffident overtures Clara expected from him. As soon as they were settled in a dim corner of a picture-house, his arm slid round her waist. The contact made her body stiffen, her mind object. She did not like the game to be taken out of her own hands. Fred's quick methods were frightening and his kisses exciting. Clara collected all her forces, but they did not function properly. Instead of growing colder as the man's ardour increased, her power of resistance lessened. She enjoyed the stimulus of Fred's caresses as fresh experience. The realisation was shattering, for it proved her not immune from the advances of men. For a time, the knowledge gained helped her to avoid Fred's desire, but in the end he had his way with her. Weak thoughts of eventual experience with men led to her acceptance of Fred's desires, though in this hour of triumph her fears returned.

After that, pride did not save her from him; a thing once known is known again in a more easy fashion. At times she felt regret for submitting so soon; she had lost more than she had gained.

Her hold on Fred was slender. Over this she raged with secret helplessness, till at last she knew that Fred, like herself, was selfish. In all things he came first. Two people cannot come first in the order of things, and as Fred liked Clara less than he liked himself, she resentfully took the place he casually allotted her as his mistress. Sometimes she would upbraid him fiercely, threatening to tell Ivy. Fred only shrugged. He told her brutally: "Ivy knows me. You are not the first woman I've gone wrong with since I married, my dear. Get on with it. Tell her. She'll only put you as far out of my company as possible. If you want a minute's notice, tell her. As it is, I'm pretty sure young Tom suspects us." Clara stared at him sullenly the first time he said such things, doubting their truth. It might be bluff; she wished that she could think it was. To accept the fact that Fred cared so little for her was a miserable necessity, but it had to be done. Future affairs would gain a sounder foundation as a result of such bitter experience. Other men should pay for Fred's careless treatment. For Ivy, her contempt grew: a woman who allowed her husband to behave in the light way Fred did, did not deserve one. Ivy's conduct seemed more scandalous than Fred's. For hours Clara brooded in her bedroom.

To-night she would know definitely about her condition. If what she thought had happened, well, Fred would have to do something. She hoped her fears were wrong. If they were wrong, she would go from Grovelace with Fred, or without him, leaving a pretty scandal behind. If she went alone, the folks at the Greyhound should know what she thought of them first. She ached to pour her feelings of contempt on Ivy; all the venom in her nature rose at the thought. And the landlady's brother, he, too, should hear a few things about himself. Dirty little spy. Tom was the only man she had ever met at close quarters who failed to respond to her charms and delicate overtures. For that she hated him. She had not desired him except as a scalp for her collection, but his failure to respond infuriated her. At first, supposing him shy, she gave him subtle encouragement. When the boy became conscious of her interest, his coldness turned to scarcely veiled hostility. So provoked, her own feelings quickly turned to hatred. Everything that she could do to widen the rift between the lad and his brother-in-law was done. Fred's dislike for Tom seemed to be the only emotion he held deeply; the boy was at the bottom of all the trouble between Ivy and himself. Ivy free from such an influence would be much more easy to deal with.

Clara wondered if Fred would understand the full import of her letter. She hoped so, though it did not much matter. Whatever happened, she would see him after time.

George Phips was anxious to have her. She might take him. He would be none the wiser till it was too late. The prospect of life married to a miner was not tempting, nothing like her dreams. George was all right, a bit slow though. The only thing he ever bought her was a drink on Saturday night. Miners did not make much money these days. If she took him there would soon be a houseful of squalling children, she herself dragged down by them. He might turn nasty when he learnt the truth about her, too.

No, if Fred would do nothing for her, she would clear out of Grovelace as soon as ever things were straight. Fred would do something. He must. She would make him, somehow.

Clara took a little box from a drawer in the dressing-table; it held the jewellery she got out of Fred. There was a string of white coral beads, a gold wrist-watch, and his latest gift, a brooch with green stones set in an oval of gold. Fastening it, the pin caught her throat, drawing a thin line of blood there. Clara shuddered. It was a sign of misfortune, unlucky.

She was going to see a wise woman, Bedelia Gee, an old crone who lived by herself in a tumble-down cottage on the Grovedon estate. The old woman was very clever.

Widow Hacks said she talked with the devil. Clara did not believe that, but Bedelia was clever as everyone knew. When the doctor's back was turned she was always fetched to a child-bed; it was she who presided over the rite of couvade.

When Clara was born, old Asa refused to play the part, refusing to get in her mother's bed or let her lie against his breast. Mary Ann Tapin raged weakly against him, even going down on her knees to plead, but Asa would not yield to her wishes. Bedelia predicted an awful future for the girl child, so Mrs. Tapin spent two of the Squire's golden pounds in buying her daughter a potent charm against Asa's evil wishes. Clara laughed. Surely a thing like that could not help her, yet it might. She searched in her drawer till she found the charm-containing pouch, which she fastened by a string round her neck. It was best to be on the safe side.

Supposing Bedelia was entertaining visitors—she might be. Clara hoped not; she wanted to know the worst at once, not to be kept in horrid suspense. She put on her hat, anxious to be gone, yet dreading to go.

Mrs. Flack said she might have an extra half-hour off duty, so there was no need to hurry; there would be time to nip home first.

The lamp was lit and the fire burnt brightly in her mother's kitchen. Old Asa sat there; he did not say a word to her, but only scowled. Surly old swine. Childishly she stuck her tongue out at him. "Respect grey hairs, daughter of an whore," he reproved her sternly. She squealed with laughter, taunting him, "Bald-headed old coot," her voice shrill with hate. Mrs. Tapin came down the stair ladder. She and Clara talked in quiet whispers so that the old man should not hear what they talked of. The Tapin household was never at peace. Both man and wife sought in every way to disturb and annoy each other. Clara had never known any other atmosphere but that of bitter hatred. Asa's tiny pension barely kept the house going, yet no matter how bad the times were, he kept his own spending money back. To get a little pleasure for herself and the girl, Mrs. Tapin turned her hand to any work, good or evil, that would bring in a few pence.

The girl's childhood was a time of misery and bitterness. Because of her great pride, other children did not like her. She despised them; in return they made her suffer. She read on the lavatory walls of Straycross School: "Clara Tapin's a bastard." They jeered at her on the way home from school, screaming filthy words after her. When she left school, her hard beauty increased and the lads sought her eagerly; then she got her revenge. The girls found she could attract their boys with a wink of the eye. The boys she excited, to spurn later. She hated the Grovedons, Asa and the village people; the feeling she knew for her mother did not go deep.

Till she met Fred, George Phips was the only man she liked at all. Clara got up from the fireside suddenly, "See you later, Ma," she said, and was gone.

V

AN insistent hammering sound disturbed Freddy's sleep. He woke up. There were men in the tap-room needing beer. It was time he got up. It was a pity if Ivy, Clara and Tom could not attend to customers' wants without his help for half an hour. The recognised sound stopped: that meant the tankards were being collected for refilling.

Remembering it was Saturday night, Freddy forgot the unpleasant thoughts with which he awoke. Stretching delightfully, he wished Ivy was beside him. Women were the very deuce; he could not resist them. Fortunately he knew how to treat them. Time given to the study of individual women always repaid him. The thought made him chuckle. The way in which old Aunt Susan responded to his wheedling tricks had saved his backside from many a tanning. A bit of thought, and any woman could be got round.

If only men could be got round in the same fashion, life would be very pleasant, but men were different, worse luck. Still, men had their points: they could make an appreciative audience for his tales, they could give him tips on horse-racing, spend money in his pub; besides, he liked men. It was funny the difference between men and women. Women, he liked women, and of all those he had ever known, Ivy came first. She was a good sort, easy-going and nice, though she did nag at times. That was young Tom's fault mostly. Why couldn't the lad be more cheerful? Worry never did anybody good. Besides, it upset Ivy. If the boy would only clear out, he and Ivy would come through the rough time smiling. The trouble with young Tom lay in the fact of him being a born mischief-maker. For Ivy's sake, Freddy wanted to like the boy; it was the lad's own fault that they didn't get on very well together. After all, no man was going to stand interference in his own house from a slip of a lad like young Tom. The sooner Tom got that into his head the better it would be for everyone. If he only knew it, he had come very close to a darn good hiding many times for his saucy remarks; only his being Ivy's brother saved him. Freddy pondered the matter over. The boy was frightened of him, he felt pretty certain about that. When Ivy was out, there was never any impudence. At such times the lad went quietly about the place, keeping a still tongue in his head. It might be worth trying: next time Ivy went to Chesterfield, he would take Tom in the backyard. If there was a stand-up fight, so much the better; if not, he would give Master Tom a good old-fashioned leathering. If that did not improve matters the boy must go. Freddy smiled to himself, pleased with such a conception of brotherly conduct towards Tom.

After that the boy would know who was master, and a word delicately allusive would be enough to bring him to order. There had been enough messing about; he was sick of it. Ivy must get rid of Clara. The girl was getting a darn nuisance with her whining threats; he was tired of her too, almost. She had better go. Ivy was pretty smart as a rule in catching him out, but so far Clara skilfully kept their meetings secret. Young Tom guessed, not much doubt about that. What had Clara got against the lad? No use wondering. Women were so darn funny in their likes and hates. The best thing to do for himself would be to keep Clara down the cellar some time till Ivy came to look for her or himself. That would settle Clara's hash, once and for all.

The rowing Ivy might give him would soon dissolve with Clara gone. He rather liked the look of Mrs. Hickman's Gertie; she was a meek sort. Anyway he was sick of long-tongued women. It would be easy to dodge Clara once she was out of the house. Not much fun having two women fond of him under the same roof; it was a mug's game. Clara had only herself to blame. Fancy her being daft enough to think he would do a bunk with her. The idea was absurd. He was quite happy at the Greyhound, even though trade was bad; when it bucked up Ivy's temper would grow sweet. There was no need to worry yet.

It was not as though they owed the brewers anything yet. When all the deposit money was gone, Ivy would have cause to worry, but not until. Women got the wind up over nothing. All that fuss she made over the few drinks he gave away, as if it would not bring more custom to the house in the long run. The dull countryfolks needed showing how to enjoy life. Already they were waking up; glad to slip in for an odd drink out of hours, or stay on for a game of cards in the evening. As for drinking too much, how would she like him to get drunk every night, instead of once a week? It was all work and no play that made the Grovelace villagers so dull. The miners from Scrutton way were a bit more lively. They made Saturday night something to look forward to. Apart from the comfort of living in a pub, life was a bit dull weekdays, especially if Ivy wore a long face. When she started prophesying misfortune, it got on his nerves, and they rowed. It was a mistake to row in front of Tom; the poor fool had no idea of the power he had over Ivy. And she might rave her head off, but in the end he would do just as he liked. Always he had done so. The woman was not born who could make him alter; she never would be. It was about time Ivy knew that much, too. She might be more reasonable then.

In giving him life Freddy's mother died. The only two people of any importance during childhood were Aunt Susan and his father. The boy's parent was hard and distant; there had not been any great affection between them. To his aunt, a spinster of thirty-five, Freddy was affectionate. The woman worshipped him; he was the only living thing in which she took pleasure. No matter what trouble he got into, she found an excuse for him. All the money she could scrape from the housekeeping allowance went to buy him quickly discarded toys. She was grateful if he showed sufficient interest to destroy them. In catering for the household, his likes were considered first, and his greediness she valued as a tribute to her skill. When at last he was obliged to go to school, she did her best to make Mr. Flack write the headmaster that on no account might Freddy be caned. Her brother smiled grimly and refused her. "No, Susan, you've spoilt the boy long enough. If he earns the stick at school, he'll get it, I hope, hard and often on the proper place." Miss Flack retired crestfallen: the boy was going where she could not shield him. A strong desire for popularity, and a distinct aptness for games, won Freddy a certain amount of success among his school-fellows. With his masters he was often in trouble. They liked him well enough, but his school work was poor.

Mr. Flack took a grim delight in teasing his sister over the boy's school report that gave a list of crimes for which Freddy had been punished during the term. When Freddy was fifteen his father died. By that time he had grown very sturdy, and was nearly six feet tall.

His aunt never tired of looking at him. Freddy was going to be a very handsome man. Really handsome, with his fair complexion and vivid eyes. His mouth was a little slack, but not many people would notice that. Miss Flack found in him her ideal man; broad-shouldered and slim, his proud bearing and arrogant manner were, she felt, supremely masculine. To wait on him hand and foot seemed only his due; she did it willingly, and he let her. Without Mr. Flack's wages it was hard to look after his comfort properly, but she did her best.

Freddy thoroughly enjoyed life without his father's interference. On his sixteenth birthday he left school, and after a couple of months spent knocking around on his own, he got a job in a shoe shop. Because he was not punctual he received notice after being there six weeks. Job after job was gained and lost in the same fashion. Freddy did not care about work, though some had to be done to keep him in pocket-money. One thing, Birmingham was a big place, and he could always find work when he set out to look for it. He liked change.

When he was eighteen he joined the army for the duration of the war. Owing to a defect of eyesight he was found unfit for service abroad. After his first disappointment wore off, he managed to have a fairly good time on home service. Shortly after he was demobilised his aunt died. She left him all her money and furniture. He sold everything.

Possessing six hundred and forty pounds, he decided to enjoy himself. Fred found enjoyment impossible on his own. The girl he bought cigarettes from he thought rather a sport. She jumped at his suggestion of a gay time in London. They lived together quite happily for six months. At the end of that time only twenty pounds of his aunt's money remained after he had paid the hotel bill and given the girl a five-pound note.

They went back to Birmingham on different trains.

Life in rooms, without Aunt Susan to look after him, he found beastly. Then he met Ivy. She was a smart girl; he liked her. The idea of marriage was novel. Ivy would be able to look after him, spoil him in the same way that Aunt Susan had. It would be fun to own a publican for father-in-law. That meant a drink out of hours whenever he liked. And Ivy, she was a good kid. It flattered his self-conceit to find her so responsive to his love-making.

Most women responded to his lightest overture; he enjoyed seeking such tributes to his own charm. Ivy was proud of it too, though she was furious if he showed too much interest in another woman. That amused Fred; he was a born philanderer, liking variety in everything. Rolling out of bed, he fumbled for matches, lit the lamp and found a cigarette. He stalked about the bedroom naked, enjoying the touch of cool air on his body. All his best clothes lay out neatly on the chest. Ivy must have done that. After a wash Freddy commenced to dress quickly. He cleared all the pockets of his working-clothes, then picked up Clara's note. He'd better see what the wench wanted.

"Dear Fred,
"Am seeing B. G. to-night. Will tell you all news later. A. T.

"Clara."

Fred could guess what the news would be, he chuckled. That girl still saw in him an eloping lover. Well, she would soon find out her mistake. She no longer possessed his desire. If she was quiet and sensible, he would stay friendly, an occasional kiss and bit of fun should reward her. If she played up for a row, she would find a bigger one than she expected. He did not care much which way she blew, cold or hot, his wife was always there in the background. Sometimes Ivy threatened to leave him, but that was as far as it got. Threats hurt no one.

After all, the world was full of women. He would be sorry if Ivy did leave him eventually; still, he could quickly find someone else.

He expected her to make a terrible row if she learnt the truth about the amount owing to the brewers. More than half her capital had vanished during their six months' tenancy of the public-house. The place ate up money, though there was always a little in the till from which he could help himself.

Tom acted treasurer for the takings; he went to Chesterfield to pay into the bank what remained of the week's takings each Friday. It was only a few pounds each week, and things like the tobacconists' and the mineral water manufacturers' bills were paid from that account each month. The brewery received a small cheque too. Fred doubted if they had banked enough during February to meet the bills that would soon be in again. The brewery would have to wait, that was all.

It would do no good to alarm Ivy by telling her how money matters stood.

Things might improve; they were bound to as the year progressed. In these days of motor traffic, people would take a chance of exploring the Straycross road. The Greyhound was an attractive little pub, typical of North Derbyshire, built of dark grey stone. The bright curtains Ivy hung the windows with would show motoring folks that the Greyhound possessed a superior type of innkeeper.

SATURDAY NIGHT AT THE GREYHOUND

Fred became very cheerful as he pictured the rosy future. There were all sorts of improvements he could devise when business improved, and he could do most of them himself. Good improvements were sound investments, for they increased the house's valuation price.

He laughed, thinking of the day on which they took the house over. Burnham tried to persuade him to take to all sorts of old rubbish, but he refused to. The outgoing man got so annoyed with him, especially over the hens. Burnham wanted half a crown apiece for them; he offered two shillings. In the end Burnham twisted the neck of every bird, and drove away from Grovelace looking like a poultry-monger. It had been a great joke, though in the end the laying pullets he bought of Joe Grinds cost him two-and-nine a bird.

In front of the wardrobe glass he paused and set his tie-pin straight. There was no mistake he looked very smart in his riding-breeches and well-tailored coat. Quite the country gentleman. He lit a fresh cigarette and hummed gaily. Saturday was the best day in the week. Folks came in with money to burn. He would encourage them all right.

The men in the tap-room were making more noise now. They would be pleased to see him, since last weekend he had got hold of two or three new stories for them. He laughed coarsely. There was bound to be some fun. Saturday night was the best of the week.

PART TWO
THE OPEN HOUSE

I

THE rain had stopped. Over the hillside towards Chesterfield odd lights twinkled from lonely cottages. From his vantage-point at the Greyhound door Tom could see them. He turned, looking towards a cluster of lights that proved the existence of Grovelace village. A wind came touching him harshly; at last, shivering, he retreated into the passage. In the tap-room a good fire burnt, sending out popping sparks. He stood back to it considering the naked ugliness of the room. From the smoke-blackened ceiling an old-fashioned lamp hung. The floor was of uneven dull-grey flags; he could feel the cold of them through the thin soles of the old dancing-pumps he had on. Four narrow tables of scrubbed deal bore the marks of a thousand nights' drinking. Neither soap nor scrubbing would utterly remove those ringed stains. On each of the brown-painted walls hung a garish advertisement of someone's whisky or cigarettes. At one side of the room stood a set of table skittles, a dart board, and a wooden box containing dominoes and draughts. In Grovelace, dominoes was a popular game for those skilled in cheating. Old Pike was so expert a deceiver that strangers were the only people that he could induce to play with him for aught but the love of the game. A low cupboard stood in the cleft of the fireplace. Low schoolboy forms guarded two sides of each table. Tom suddenly remembered the spittoons. He lit a candle from the kitchen fire and went down to the cellar for sawdust. When the black-leaded circles had been disposed of, he went into the serving bar. The waiting for custom he found tedious, so different from the towns, where men stood waiting on a public-house doorstep at the moment of opening. It was on that account Freddy deserted the service bar. Tom knew, refusing to be deceived by his brother-in-law's flattery: "You've got the experience." Still he did not mind, indeed he was glad, for his place behind the service counter won respect for him from the Greyhound patrons. For his qualities of work and aloofness they admired him too; he was far more fitted to occupy the position of landlord than the boastful, too-familiar Freddy. In spite of Mrs. Tapin's suggestive hints, the villagers had, in judging the tenants of the Greyhound, found most virtue in Tom. He in turn gained respect for them. They were difficult to understand, these people; their hard exterior hostility was something he had never met before. The gaunt countryside was reflected in their grim faces. Suffering and poverty made them hard and callous in their speech, though drink betrayed them as sentimental. Always on Saturday evening they sang old songs, preferring the mawkish type. Even the children possessed no pity; the harshness of life eliminated it from them. At first Tom thought them animals, their fierceness frightened him. They laughed harshly at stories of cruelty that turned him sick. In spite of all, he admired them; their persistent struggle to gain the means of their existence was great in its way.

There was not one of them with whom he would have changed places; sooner he would have died.

Most of the men kept whippets; one or two, like Freddy, kept greyhounds. Tom found the dogs symbolic; they had hardness and the firm tenacity of their masters. They were not like other dogs, always expressing joy and devotion to their lordly owner, man. Dog, like master, had affection in his grim nature. Unlike other dogs who hunt in mad scampering, hither-and-thither fashion, the whippet goes straight, with the deadly certainty of a bullet, to the quarry. All the dog owners poached with brazen slyness. On Sunday gangs of miners would come in from Scrutton, their pockets bulging; the dogs came watchfully, each close on his master's heels. In the tap-room they sat discussing their morning's sport, the dogs lying in quiet alertness at their feet. Many a man found his dog more valuable than his wife; most of the dogs were treated as though indeed they were. Woe betide the small boy caught mauling his father's dog, a savage beating was his punishment.

A door swung open, and a gust of wind fled up the dim passage clattering the tin wall advertisements. Tom answered the noise with his presence. Two men, villagers, had come; he served them with tankards of beer and returned to the bar.

Ivy was there, her stool drawn close to the fire. They discussed the weather and its influence on trade. March was coming in lion-like, if present signs could be trusted. Collecting a trayful of glass mugs, Tom put them on a small round table near Ivy; he drew a stool close and commenced to polish them. Ivy was beginning to look her age. There were lines at her eyes; she looked tired, ill. She wore a black skirt of some heavy silk stuff and a knitted black silk jumper. She asked, "How's the time, Tom?" The boy looked at his wrist-watch, answering, "Ten past six. Gould and Willet are in the tap-room, no one else. Where's Fred?" Ivy snorted. It hurt her pride to think that Fred was not down, though for other reasons she was glad. She said shortly, "In bed as usual, lazy swine."

Tom got up, stretching, walked behind the bar counter and started the alarm-clock going. He looked at

Ivy doubtfully. "Don't you think you'd better give him a shout?" he suggested. The woman shook her head violently, her voice angry. "I shan't. I wish he'd sleep till ten. He won't though, not him. As soon as he hears them banging on the tap-room tables he'll be down." She put the polished glasses away, nodding her head emphatically. "The first sound he hears of the tap-room lot he'll get up." "And get tight," her brother sneered, sniffing with contempt.

Ivy agreed in a dull voice. "I suppose he will. He's never yet kept sober through a Saturday night since we've been here." Tom went white. The week before he and Albert Sherman had carried Fred up to his bedroom dead drunk half an hour before closing time. His hatred flamed up; he said deliberately, "I wish he'd fall down the cellar steps and break his neck. He won't, though. No such luck." The words shocked Ivy; she knew the feeling that existed between Freddy and Tom, but she could not bear it to come out naked and ugly through speech. She gazed at Tom reproachfully and said seriously, "Don't talk like that, Tom. Drunken men and babies fall soft, though . . . It might do him good, frighten him like."

From the tap-room came the clang of a tankard thumping the table. Tom went along and served the order. "Where's Clara?" he asked sharply, on going back to the bar. Ivy smiled; she wished Fred thought as little of the girl as Tom did. She told him, "I said she need not come on duty till half-past." Tom was satisfied with her answer; he suggested hopefully, "Why not get rid of her and her mother? If they and Freddy cleared out, you and me could make a do of things here. Freddy never ought to have come in this business. You made a bad mistake, old girl." Ivy nodded. It was true, but she defended herself. "He wanted to come; he jumped at the idea. I talked hard at him, trying to explain, and he promised me that when we got here he'd give up the drink; nearly." "Nearly." The boy echoed her last word scornfully. Ivy repeated stubbornly, "Nearly. Yes, he said he would only drink what customers bought him. That's what he said. I thought he meant it. I did hope he meant it, Tom." The boy nodded; his pity for her did not restrain the bitterness he held against her husband. "As it is, he buys drink for all the ragtag and bobtail in the whole blinking district! No wonder they don't spend much here, with him giving the stuff away half the time." Ivy saw the logic of that; it was against all her training and experience, the foolish way in which Freddy gave people free beer. In a landlord it was ridiculous, unheard of. She said despairingly, "I know, I can't stop him. What would you do?" A frown deepened on Tom's brow; desperate measures were needed. He snarled savagely, "Hit him on the head with a mallet. Before long he'll have D.T.'s, Ivy; no man can go on the way he does. And by that time you'll be ruined. How much does he owe the brewery?"

The fire drew Ivy; she leaned forward holding her hands to the warmth. Her brother's question made her cold; fear nagged at her. That was something she dare not think about. Fred was such a liar. Sometimes he mentioned one figure, sometimes another; she was not sure, she could not be sure.

Tom repeated, "How much, Ivy?" She faced him nervously, answering, "Ninety-five pounds, I think it is, Tom." The boy shrugged his shoulders. If Fred had told Ivy that huge amount, it was sure to be over. The valuation was only two hundred and fifty. Ruin was upon them; he could do nothing for them. If Ivy left Fred, that would be different. Together they could start an eating-house somewhere near the Birmingham Bull Ring. Why hadn't Ivy taken Arthur Wilkins? He voiced the question. Ivy did not really know; Arthur had been a nice lad, but he lacked Fred's attractiveness. That was the answer. "He did not treat me like Fred did." Her brother laughed shortly. Women were all the same, daft when it came to judging a man. A fine body and pretty ways got them every time.

Ivy, too, thought of her husband as a lover. He'd been such a nice chap when they courted, and mad about herself. Suddenly she burst out passionately, "I wish I hated him, Tom; I wish I hated him, but I can't. If only he'd try. We'd do well in the summer. What with teas and that. Food's nearly all profit." That story Tom had heard before, but summer would not find them at the Greyhound. God alone knew where they'd be then. He fumbled in his trouser pocket and found a scrap of crumpled paper which he handed across to Ivy.

"That's Grinds's receipt; he was pleased to get it, though he didn't say 'thank you'. I dare say he'll stop shouting the odds now." Smoothing out the piece of paper, Ivy read: "Dr. to Samuel Grinds, 30/9 for two prize hens and a turkey. Paid Saml. Grinds." She questioned: "Did he say anything about it?" The boy answered, "'Bout time, too. I'd a got somebody to knock that dog of his on the head if you'd not brought it soon." Putting the receipt in her purse, Ivy commented shortly, "Fred's a fool. It did us a bit of no good in the village, owing that poor old cripple thirty bob." "Of course it did," agreed Tom angrily. "But you couldn't make Fred see that. That damn dog of his. Two hens and a turkey in one night; it's never brought home a hare or a rabbit yet." Going to the door Ivy called softly, "Naxi, Naxi." The dog came quickly, its proud head borne on too slender shoulders. It would never catch a rabbit, for she and Fred spoilt it, she knew that. Wrapt up in Pertinax, lay her fortune, Ivy felt. A chain of slight coincidences made her believe firmly in the dog's virtue as mascot to the inn. His very breed and her first sight of the animal made Ivy want him. Its owner, seeing her eagerness to possess the dog, rooked Freddy over the deal. She resented that on her husband; it was a bad omen. She failed to see that Fred had bought it to please her chiefly. Tom and she had known the greyhound was faulty, not worth half the sum Fred paid for him. From a breeder's point of view the animal should have been destroyed. That made Fred furious; the dog was a wonder. Instead of giving Ivy the dog, he kept it for himself, extolling its many virtues and maintaining that he had bought it cheaply. In spite of this, they were all fond of Naxi. The dog had beauty in their eyes, though on most showing points he was underdeveloped, and had the naughty vice of chicken-killing.

The Grovelace villagers watched, amused; they all knew Pertinax and his tricks. Every time a fowl met with accidental death, its owner would carry it bleeding up to the Greyhound, accusing Naxi and demanding compensation. Fred soon tired of that and kept the dog chained up. Then one night he got away; several people saw him hanging round Grinds's place. Next morning the old cobbler came up the hill in his wheeled chair, a bloody cargo of mangled flesh and feathers with him. The landlord denied liability, and the old man, already in a furious rage, threatened what would happen to Naxi. The villagers, having enjoyed making Fred pay for the damage done by rats and other enemies of poultry, were incensed at his refusal to pay the cripple.

This was a genuine case. Naxi was known to be a killer, and old Grinds had an extra hard time of things. Ivy and Tom took the cripple's side, too; it was only right and just that he should be paid. Fred remained obstinate; he had said he would not pay, and no one could make him. Ivy, because of her pity for the cripple, and her fear that some horrid vengeance might be Naxi's fate, took the money out of the till and gave it to Tom. The bill paid and Naxi, naughty dog, was safe, she felt.

Tom asked, "Did he miss it?" In her dream, stroking the pet's silken coat, Ivy was startled. "Miss what?" she said. "The money you took out of the till to pay Grinds with?" Ivy shook her head. "No. That proves what a fool he is. It would not be safe to leave him alone in the house for half a day," her brother said. That was true enough; if Tom was out she had to stay in.

Freddy was like a young child: he craved the importance of responsibility, but was utterly unfitted for it; like a child he believed himself able to do anything. In spite of his powerful body, his fierce blustering manner, if any trouble arose in the tap-room between the patrons, it was not he who quelled it but his wife or brother-in-law. In an argument he made the mistake of taking sides with some of the men involved. Tom, in spite of his smallness, tackled the trouble with impartial friendliness and grim determination. "If you want to fight, fight, but wait till you get outside," he would shout, pushing in between two close, angrily threatening men, shoving them apart with his puny strength, insisting, "Shut up, or out you go."

Brother and sister sat in silence, gazing at the fire. The lack of custom worried them both. Business was rotten. The only people who drew wages from the Greyhound were the Tapins, mother and daughter. For the first few weeks Tom had been paid a small sum each Friday night, then Freddy said, hoping the boy would clear out, "Sorry, Tom, I can't afford to pay you any wages; trade's too bad." "I'll stay without, then," was the boy's answer.

Later he and Ivy talked things over. She could not do without him. That touched him like a caress; as long as Ivy wanted him he would stay. The love he had for her renewed itself in her need; now by his faithfulness, by sacrifice, he might prove to himself the sincerity of his love. Ivy declared madness would overtake her if Tom went; she took his head on her shoulder, kissing him, weeping in passionate gratitude. Often she proffered the lad a few shillings she had taken from the till. To aid her self-respect he took them; they were added to his savings. Tom's own needs were small; he smoked a little, and spent a half-day every week in Chesterfield. He had plenty of clothing, and his work provided food and lodging.

Tom sat up and looked at the clock. "It's time Clara was back," he commented, then inquired, "Is it true what they say about her being Squire Grovedon's daughter?" Ivy looked up, her face hard. She replied, "I should think so; she has airs enough for a countess. Little bitch, she encourages Fred, I'm sure of it. You wait. I'll catch 'em together yet, then out she'll go, the little strumpet." "What makes you so sure about Fred and her?" asked the boy. Ivy glowered, muttering: "Never you mind. I've reasons, good ones. And I'm not the fool they both take me to be, not by a long chalk."

Fury had flung colour into Ivy's cheeks; she got to her feet, walking up and down the room. Tom watched her sympathetically. Ivy was suffering an agony of jealousy, that strange fever which drives men and women insane, the force that betrays its victim. Tom knew her pain but could not help her. In herself lay the remedy. "Poor Ivy," he thought, his rage mounting against his brother-in-law. Suddenly Ivy paused in her walk, and stood, head on one side, listening. Lifting her head, she whispered, "Here she comes." Clara walked in, her face pale, her mouth set. She looked round, then asked, "Where's the boss" Without looking up, Tom said, "Where the hell d'yer think?" The girl moved rapidly towards him, her face working. She stood over him and said tensely, "Who do yer think you're talking to? I'm not standing your sauce, even if you are the Missus's brother." Tom stared at her in contempt. He stood up, and commenced, "Why, I'll say what——" "Shut up, Tom," interposed Ivy, quickly. She turned to Clara with great dignity, and said, "It's nothing to do with you, Clara, where Mr. Flack is." Clara opened her mouth as though to speak, then turned, walking haughtily out of the bar. Tom grinned, observing, "You soon shut her up." But Ivy's rage still held. Her voice trembled. "I'll get them yet, Tom, her and Fred. Then out she'll go, bag and baggage." The boy laughed. "Eh, she is that; it'll be good riddance to bad rubbish when she goes." Ivy laughed, too, harshly, her face wild. The thought of Clara in Fred's arms hurt her badly. In her heart she blamed the girl, exonerating Freddy. She liked to believe him an easy though unwilling victim. She had made a mistake in not sending the girl away before. The moment she suspected Fred was attracted by Clara's youthful charm would have been the time to act. If her suspicions were correct, Fred would not dare to have said anything. But having let that moment pass, she must wait now till she caught them out.

Freddy came in. He had slept well, and was ready for

an evening's fun. To both Ivy and Tom he was well disposed. They were not so bad. In the end they would realise he was not going to stand any interference. Then they would behave. He knew Ivy; when Clara got the chuck he would make up to her, then Master Tom would see for himself who the boss really was. Freddy chuckled; he beamed on Tom, asking, "Everything ready, Tommy? Got that barrel of four X tapped?" The boy nodded. "Yes, and I've filled up the barrel of old." Fred rubbed his hands together and winked slyly; the sharp practices of Tom and Ivy connected with the house delighted him. He loved to think of the odd coppers they made by collecting "swipes" and tap drippings. If they would have let him carry it out, he had evolved a plan of doping the beer with burnt sugar water. But Ivy put her foot down firmly on that idea, Tom supporting her. They had a wholesome respect for the excise officer. Many get-rich-quick friends of the Birmingham days had got into trouble that way. The tricks of the trade were both useful and profitable to those who knew where the line must be drawn. Compared with Fred, she and Tom were experts; if he thought he could teach them anything new he was mistaken.

Fred was happy. "We'll make a fortune yet," he declared. "Not till you give up the booze," Ivy told him coldly. "Why don't you, Fred?" put in Tom, eagerly. "You've no call to go buying drinks for all the blasted regulars, either." Freddy turned on the boy furiously, the smile gone from his face. "Mind your own damn business. If you don't like it, you can get out." It was just like them to start on him. He came down feeling in a high good humour with himself and the world, and they must needs pick on him. "Clear out," he repeated angrily, scowling. Ivy said firmly, "If Tom goes, Fred,

I'll go too. You're the laughing-stock of the whole place. You fool, you think they're fools, don't you? But you're the fool. Folks who drag a living from the earth like they do aren't daft. Not by a long chalk. You're the mug." Tom got up and went out. He hated rows, yet by his presence he provoked both Ivy and Fred. In front of him they said bitter, hateful things. He tried not to take sides; to be impartial, but that was impossible. Apart from any question of relationship, Ivy's case always seemed right and fair, Fred's wrong and bad. For Ivy's sake it might be better if he took Fred's unbidden advice and left. He could get a job in London or Birmingham quite easily. He could go back to the Bristol and take on his work there; when Ivy needed him, he could be there, waiting for her. She would not want him to go. If Fred were a little better, a little more likely to make a success of living at the Greyhound, he would go back to London in spite of Ivy's pleas. . . . Fred would come a cropper eventually. He had better stay in the bar.

Ivy taunted her husband: "You're the mug." He glared at her, then at the door through which Tom had gone. "Shut your mouth," he ordered her, his voice thick. "You and your blasted brother, you make me sick. First one and then the other. I'm sick of the pair of you."

Going behind the bar counter, he reached down a bottle of whisky and poured out a stiff drink. After adding a little water from a jug on the counter, he drank it at a gulp. Ivy watched him reproachfully. Bitterly she said, "Not half as sick as I am of you. Can't you see that the folks here have got you weighed up? That Dick Barle was in here this morning. Said as you owed him two quid. Won it off you at banker, he said. He asked me to give it him." Fred wiped the back of his hand across his mouth. "Did you?" he asked, anxiously. Ivy sneered. "Give it him? Why, there weren't two quid in the till. Dirty little swine. I'm not afraid of him. I gave him a piece of my mind, though." Her husband grinned. He was much relieved. What he did not pay at the actual time of losing he never paid later. "That's all right, then," he told Ivy.

"But it's not all right," she said, her voice earnest, beseeching. "Oh, Fred, I do wish you would give up the drink. Don't have much to-night."

He turned on her, his face livid. "Shut your bloody mouth, for Heaven's sake."

Ivy gasped; she was white and trembling. "Oh, you fool, you fool," she told him passionately.

Snatching the water-jug from the counter, Fred flung it at her, shouting: "Now, will you shut up?" He gazed at her vacantly as she cowered against the floor, her clothes sodden with water, the broken pieces of pottery round her knees. The crash brought Tom hurrying in. He went to Ivy, raising her from the ground. In the doorway Clara stood watching. Another row. So much the better. Fred might be all the more kind to herself. Cautiously she made a signal to him, but he could not have seen, for he walked out of the room whistling. A moment later she heard him greet the tap-room customers, "Hello, boys, how goes it?" in a cheerful voice.

Clara returned to the lonely smoke-room, a smile hovering round her mouth. Popularity Freddy loved better than he loved any woman. She could tell him some of the things she had heard hard-headed folks in the village say of him. He would be too vain to believe them. He would merely turn against her. She played with her beads, anxious for customers to come in. Sitting alone served to increase her misery; she twisted her beads till they broke, rattling down on to the floor. Getting down on her knees, she picked up all she could find and put them in a scrap of paper.

II

THE quarrel upset Ivy. For some minutes after Fred left she remained shaking as she sat in helpless uncontrol. Tom knelt by her, patting her with gentle hands, trying to give her comfort. At last she stood up. "I'll go and change," she told Tom briefly.

When she had gone he cleared away the mess. There ought to be people in soon. When everything was straight he picked up the evening paper and commenced to read. Presently Clara came to the smoke-room door again and stared. Lifting his head, Tom scowled at her. She retreated without speaking. Old Asa Tapin came in. "'Night," he gave Tom, curtly; the boy echoed him. Asa was his most regular customer. He came in every evening about seven o'clock; he liked to be sure of the fireside seat. Asa was a queer sort of man; he did not talk much. If he made a remark, Tom always found something caustic or bitter in it. Old Asa disliked his fellow-man. Tom never heard him say a kindly thing of anyone. Still, he knew where he was with the old man. On Saturday night Asa paid for five half-pints of bitter, on other nights four. He never bought anyone else a drink, though he would accept one in a surly, ungracious way. The moment Tom called time, Asa lifted the tankard to his lips, swallowing the last precious drain. Then, with a surly "'Night," he would get up and go.

With a swift jerk of the pump Tom drew the old man's beer. Asa counted the copper coins out into his hand without a word of thanks. Tom looked round the service bar with pride; though small it was neat and smart, less dingy than the other public rooms. It was his own department; he did all the rough work in connection with it. The shelves were laden with bottles of various coloured liquids. He liked to keep a good stock on show. There were dozens of highly polished glasses of every size and shape, stacks of cigarettes that mounted ceilingward like sky-scrapers. On the top shelf, alone in glory, stood a half-bottle of Benedictine, not yet opened. The miners, when they turned to fancy drinks, bought either advocat or port and brandy. The advocat was most popular; he could sell them a tiny glass of it for tenpence. They enjoyed it greatly, sipping it with slow lips; for them to indulge in it was the height of luxury and fast living. Port and brandy cost one shilling and fourpence. It braced people up, made them gay quickly. All the miners knew those drinks and their values. They were rarely tempted by the strange concoctions of gin and vermouth Tom offered to make for them. In taste they were conservative, preferring the known to the unknown. There was only seating accommodation for eight customers in Tom's bar, so he usually had room in which to move. Only Ivy, Fred and himself were supposed to go behind the counter, though Clara used to when they were very busy. He hated to see her there, and watched her closely. Three men walked in, all regular customers; they greeted him shortly, "'Evening, Tom." One of them, a younger man, asked, "Where's Clara, lad?" It was George Phips. Tom jerked his hand in the direction of the smoke-room. "In there; you're early." George went into the smoke-room. Tom knew he was fond of Clara. He rather liked the young miner, who, he felt, was decent and straight.

Clara came to the counter; she took no notice of Asa, though she nodded to the other men. "Bottle of Guinness and a port and lemon, please," she ordered. Tom tweaked the stopper off a bottle, putting it with a glass on a tray; while he prepared the other drink, Clara poured the spume-like liquid out. When she left, he turned to the other men, impatient for their order. They seemed in no hurry; he asked them, "Well?" They laughed. Tom was a proper publican; he did not like to see people without a drink in front of them. The men ordered beer, he served them. Soon Clara was back. "George wants you to have a drink with him," she said, handing him half a crown. Tom pulled a tankard of beer; he raised it to his lips without tasting. "Thank him kindly and my best respects," he told her, giving her the change. At last they had begun. Freddy came in with a tray of empty beer jars. Tom served him swiftly. "I'm playing skittles with the men, so someone else will have to serve in the tap-room," he told Tom, loftily. Tom sneered. "You'd better tell the barmaid yourself then. She objects to taking orders from me. Ivy's upstairs, so I can't leave the bar." Freddy frowned. "Clara," he shouted; she came swiftly. He explained what he wanted her to do. Her face went sulky and she went back into the smoke-room. Having sold his own half-pint Tom put the money for it in his pocket. He usually made a little money that way at week-ends.

The house began to fill. Some women sat in the passage. They talked scandal as they drank; every now and then at some choice item they would burst into shrill laughter. They would whisper sly things to Tom as he served them. He did not like it, but it was all part of the business. Not to give offence, yet to keep up an aloof friendliness was his method. Fred hobnobbed with them; no wonder they thought him of no account. He was glad when Ivy came down. She had a roving commission, going over all of the public part of the house, giving help wherever she was needed, stopping to chat with such of the patrons as felt it became their dignity to be seen talking to the landlady. The women in the passage became more bold; one by one they sidled into the service bar.

So, Tom knew, women customers would arrive at intervals during the evening. Their ultimate goal was the smoke-room, but it took a very brazen woman to be the first to enter unless she was accompanied by a man. The tap-room was reserved exclusively for men, and during the week they seldom visited the smoke-room, where beer cost a halfpenny a pint more, and those who ordered spirits or bottled beer got the best attention. Besides her work in the smoke-room Clara served the off-licence customers who came to her window jug-and-bottle department. On Saturday nights that side of trade remained very quiet. When Mr. Sharman, the blacksmith, came in with his wife, Clara was very pleased to see them, not because she liked them; she did not, but on account of the excited George. He worried her by his constant pleading for some little token of affection. If only he could really know how she felt against him, against all men.

The Sharmans gave her surly greeting, ordering bottled stout. She need not worry any longer. Mrs. Sharman might dodge from one place to another, but her old man would not move till they turned him out.

When Ivy went into the tap-room, several men hammered their mugs on the tables; such demonstration conveyed a repeat order and saved their gruff voices. Taking up a tray Ivy collected the beer jars deftly. She took them along to the service bar for Tom to fill. She did not care for serving in the tap-room. There the men seemed to keep their natural rough hardness. In the smoke-room and bar they behaved with an affected restraint as though they were at a funeral. But in the tap-room their rough vigour alarmed her. They were utterly different from the saucy Birmingham boys, with whom she was fully able to cope. Leaning over the tables to place the mugs she often received a sly pinch or caress from rough fingers. A slapped face merely made them laugh. Her complaints to Freddy did no good. They only amused him. One man, Josh Brightman, aroused all her hatred. To-night she served him cautiously, holding her body stiffly aloof. He grinned, conscious of her repugnance, his sharp teeth gleaming. When she put out her hand for the money he seized it, holding it tightly. "Freddy!" she shouted in frantic tones. Brightman dropped her hand as Fred looked round, asking in surly tones, "What the hell is the matter now?" "It's all right," she answered in flat tones. Brightman gave a low chuckle and reached out his thick hand towards her. Ivy turned and fled as though the devil were at her heels. Saturday night was hateful. One of these days she would hit Brightman full in the face with a beer jar. Perhaps that would cure him of his tricks. Dirty swine. That's what he was, to meddle with a respectable married woman. She dare not tell Tom the truth about him. Small though he was, she felt he would try and tackle Brightman with all the rage his slender frame possessed. Brightman would delight in mauling the boy. Ivy knew his reputation; in a community where human suffering is of little account people spoke of his delight in cruelty. Lightning, his fine greyhound, they said, was fed with living rabbits, dropped straight into his fifty-yard run. Ivy shuddered. A man like Brightman would worry her as long as she lived in Grovelace village.

She went into the smoke-room and sat with the Sharmans for a while. When the clanking of mugs started again, she ordered, "Clara, you run along; I'll be in here for a spell." She could not face Brightman again for a bit; it started her body shaking again at the very thought of it.

It was a good thing Tom did not know. Fred ought to be ashamed of himself. He should know by now that she did not complain about nothing. Next time she went into the tap-room Naxi should go with her. Two more people came in, Ben Hepple with his wife. Ivy liked them both. They were straight, decent people, possessing natural beauty of character. Ben was a shepherd working out in the open fields in all weathers. He and his wife came regularly to the Greyhound every Saturday night for an hour. Ben bought the first drink, Sara the second one. They never drank any more than the two glasses of stout bought by themselves, refusing to be treated with gracious politeness. They talked to Ivy in a friendly fashion. She felt she would like to let them know all her own troubles, but that would be unfair; they were sensitive enough to share her misery. Instead she told them of her brother, how he worked and did, all for her sake. The old couple nodded; they liked Tom.

In the service bar Tom found plenty to do, keeping the stock in order, washing glasses and keeping up a dull conversation with Asa Tapin about the year's gardening prospects. The old man was very gloomy. The year had made a bad start, and would make a worse finish. Such comments depressed Tom; his other visitors did little but echo Asa's views in monosyllables. Grovelace men did not talk much at the best of times. They liked a long pause between each comment. Tom wondered of what things they thought. Possibly of the pit, and its overhanging shadow of death. Two men had been killed since his coming to Grovelace. He would never forget seeing the grief-stricken women when he called with the wreaths that Ivy fetched from Chesterfield. They made him go in the dim parlours and touch the bodies death had touched. In each cottage he was given a cake and a cup of strong tea, forced to sit and consume while the woman told in hard-clipped phrases of the calamity that had overtaken her. In one room, nine white-faced children huddled together in silent awkwardness while their mother talked. The other woman, a young thing with a child at her breast, took him anew over the tragedy. He listened abashed by the hardness of such things.

Next day he attended the funerals with all their conscious panoply of grief; the crying, terror-stricken children, the wailing women. Sorrow-stricken he stumbled on at the slow tail of the procession, down the mile-long road to Straycross Church. Then back to one of the houses for tea. The women, being relations, combined together to provide the meal, not for economy's sake, but so that the funeral spread might be more sumptuous. Being a stranger at their feast Tom was looked after in a royal fashion. Ben Hepple, to whom he applied for correct instruction as to how he must behave both at funeral and feast, assured him it would give offence if he did not eat all he was offered, though he must on no account help himself to the last piece on any dish.

For weeks the double tragedy lingered over the Greyhound; men could neither think nor talk of anything else. They wondered, unsaying, whose turn would come next. A smoking concert was given at the Greyhound on behalf of the victims' relations. Fred behaved with wonderful kindness and generosity. Everyone came, bringing an offering. Asa Tapin only bought four half-pints that Saturday night and a half-ounce less of tobacco.

Tom smiled at the recollection. In many ways Grovelace villagers were admirable. Tom heard the noise of a motor-car pulling up outside. A minute later a tall, fair man not unlike Clara walked in. "You the landlord?" he asked. Tom explained his position. "The landlady is in there," he said, pointing to the smoke-room. With a nod of thanks the young man pushed open the door, and let it swing to behind him. In answer to his unspoken thought, Asa said significantly, "Squire." Tom gave a little whistle of surprise. What could he want at the Greyhound?

III

WHEN the car pulled up outside the Greyhound Inn with a jerk, Roy Grovedon turned to his companion gravely, and asked, "Well, which shall it be? Inn or ancestral hall?" Ruth Dorme laughed and chose once more the Inn. It might be dull, but a dust-curtained dining-room would be worse. She was starving, and could not wait till they got back to Matlock for food. A meal at the Greyhound might be amusing. It would be something to talk about. Anything, so long as it had novelty, that was the thing nowadays. People would enjoy hearing of her meal among the miners. If it proved too ghastly she could embroider it a little.

Ruth Dorme, an unmarried woman of thirty, found life rather boring in spite of her money. She was fairly clever and considered to be intellectual by her friends. Knowing that, she let it rule her life. She dare not say or do anything she considered might be traitorous to the intellect with which she allowed herself to be endowed. Few people liked her.

Acting on a sudden impulse she had fled from the gloom of London, dripping under February rains. Arriving at Matlock she decided she must be mad. The glum hotel, the stuffy provincial people who insisted on being friendly, were far worse than anything she left behind in London.

Of the stuffy people she soon disposed. Her defence of such old-established practices as prostitution and vivisection shocked them horribly. To one old woman who tried to convert her, she said bluntly: "A woman who eats lamb straight from the mother holds no right to condemn the cruelties of vivisection." The woman got up and left the lounge, her remaining arguments unexpounded. Ruth was bothered by no more friendly people the next evening. Those who had spoken before pretended not to see her. In any case she seemed destined to spend a loathsome week-end. Inspection of the hotel library discovered nothing more exciting than the works of Michael Arlen and Warwick Deeping. Her fat-headed maid had packed *Sodome et Gomorrhe* and *Prancing Nigger*. Neither of them suited her mood. Proust seemed incredibly boring and Ronald Firbank frantically irritating. When she was dressed for dinner she carried the books down to the lounge. It was crowded with people who looked weird. A mournful orchestra did its lurid best to depress her. Had her aim been certain she might have hurled a volume of *Sodome et Gomorrhe* at the conductor's head. That at least would cause a stir; the management might even request her to leave. Why had she come to the wretched place? Remembering the lines of Walter Raleigh on the human race, she felt his wishes absurd. The thing to do was to take the next train back to London. To people who were impertinent enough to inquire the reason of her abrupt return, she could explain that Matlock was a hideous mistake. They would admire her honesty. Getting up hastily she saw Roy Grovedon; he was one of the few men she really liked. He came across smiling. Over cocktails she told him candidly her private views of Matlock with special reference to the hotel. He was amused. To his invitation to dine she responded, "Not in this hotel." They decided to go for a run in his car. Roy picked up her books; after seeing the titles he hid them with his hand, and said sorrowfully, "The next time you apply for shelter at this respectable hotel they will exert their right to refuse admission." The absurd remark made her laugh. "If only they'd have done that yesterday," she mourned.

Soon the car fled beyond Matlock's jewelled streets, hurrying like a scared insect along the deserted roads. Roy did not care to talk; while driving he was part of the machine. Ruth found the quiet hum of the engine suited her mood. The headlights made an archway of light; they seemed to be careering down the endless aisle of a huge cathedral. Suddenly Ruth felt hungry. She nudged Roy gently; he pulled into the side of the road and brought the car to a standstill. The engine purred softly. Ruth waved her thin hands wildly, saying in tones of extravagant ferocity, "Roy, I am divinely hungered. Unless you find me food I shall become a cannibal." He said grimly, "That's an easy matter. The home of my childhood days is but a mile down yonder road. And even nearer lies the Greyhound Inn, a filthy pub. The haunt of miners, poachers and other local vermin. Either will feed you. Which?" "The Greyhound Inn will suit me nicely," she said, in tones of stilted refinement. "A gentleman ought to know better than to ask a youngish unmarried female to sup at his lonely mansion unchaperoned. Besides, your place will be all dust-sheets and apprehensive servants. The Greyhound, and the choice be on my own head." Roy snorted. "It will be bread, cheese and pickled onions," he warned, as the car moved off. Soon she could see the flickering lights of Grovelace and on the hill, aloof, those of the inn. Roy got out, bidding her wait while he made a few inquiries. When he disappeared into the house she got out of the car and went into the passage. A high-hung wall lamp flung an ill light down the stone-flagged passage. It was going to be too dreadful. Carelessly she bumped into an unseen figure. Flippantly she called over her shoulder, "Sorry." A man's voice answered harshly indignant, "And sod you too, you ignorant bitch." Frightened she dashed for a sudden brighter light and found Roy talking to a pleasant dark girl. He turned sharply, frowning, saying. "You should have waited, Ruth." She did not answer, but drew close to the fire, opening her brocade coat to its warmth. She smiled at the smiling woman, then turned to the room; half a dozen dark-clothed men sat there stiffly, and two ill-favoured women. They would not accept her smile as the dark woman had done. They had nothing to sell her, nor any desire to please. Roy nodded after the dark woman. "Mrs. Flack has put a fire in her sitting-room for us. Tomato soup, tinned, will be ready for us in five minutes. Will you have a drink?" Ruth nodded; she would like a gin and It, if that was obtainable. Roy went to the door, calling the order along the passage. A dark boy, not unlike the landlady, brought the drinks in. Presently a tall, fair girl appeared, announcing curtly, "Food's ready." Ruth saw her face was sullen, yet beautiful. On the way up the candle-lit stairs she asked Roy, "Who is the fair beauty?" Roy did not answer. She felt aggrieved, and teased him: "I expect you would not like me to know all that you know of Goldilocks?" Roy laughed coarsely, saying, "No matter what laws I break, the one concerning the fair Clara will be observed." Ruth giggled, begging, "Do tell me, Roy." "Well," he said frankly, "she happens to be one of my father's many natural children, though why natural I cannot understand."

Ruth was pleased they had come to the Greyhound. New experience alone made life worth while; that alone saved it from utter futility. The soup was hot; she enjoyed it. While waiting for the next course, she photographed the room on her memory. It was quaint, possessing a certain stiff formality, not unlike a stage setting. Over the fireplace hung an enlarged photo of a pleasant-faced old man, probably the landlady's father. Two huge and hideous blue vases flanked it. Ruth considered them gravely. "No wonder," she said, "the working classes do not care to use their best rooms." After a quick look round, Roy agreed. The room was obviously a museum of family happenings, the collected result of many marriages and deaths. The boy who served them below came in with a tray; he slid it on a side table, then removed the soup plates. Ruth watched him critically; from his quick, deft movements it was certain that he had learnt waiting in a good hotel. When he had gone, after having served them with an excellent omelette, she questioned Roy, who had but little information. "The boy is the landlady's brother. He gave up a job in London to join her in this venture. The landlord is a fool who drinks too much. They will probably leave this place for the workhouse."

Ruth felt an extraordinary interest in the Greyhound people. The slight knowledge Roy gave was too meagre; she suggested that he might pump the lad on his next appearance. Roy's grim look returned: Ruth did not seem to understand that in this inn class distinction would be preserved with a more rigid persistence than is used in a smart London hotel. He told Ruth quietly, "If you were dressed in a blouse and skirt, and had the social status of a Chesterfield butcher's wife, you'd be eating this meal in the Greyhound kitchen. The landlady would have her chair drawn up to the fire, and by now you'd be in full possession of all her past life and history. The boy will tell us just as much as he feels we are entitled to know. I'll try him, but you will be disappointed in the bareness of his answers." Ruth was. The boy answered all Roy's questions politely. When he had gone, leaving them with a dish of steak and chips, Ruth knew that trade was bad, the district not bad, the inhabitants of Grovelace were all right; to all other questions he had answered "Yes" or "No." She wondered would the barmaid tell them anything. Roy thought not; it gave him an idea. "If I can get hold of Mrs. Tapin, Clara's mother, she'll tell you all you want to know. There will not be much truth in it, though, for she is bound to have some bias for or against these folks." They finished the excellent meal, talking of distant affairs.

Tom's face haunted Ruth. She told Roy, "I have seen that boy before somewhere." Her interest revived. The few facts she learned from Tom and Roy did not satisfy her wish for information. Instead of returning to Matlock she would spend the night under the Greyhound's roof. She informed Roy of her intention. He laughed at first, but when he saw she was serious, he tried to make her see the absurdity of her wish. Ruth was not to be convinced; she laughed away all his arguments lightly. "To-morrow," she told him gaily, "you may come and fetch me after breakfast, then I can see your land and property by the light of day." Roy grinned, asking slyly, "In that get-up?" "Why not?" she countered. "The landlady will lend me a hat." Roy gave up trying to dissuade her, feeling her determination was unalterable. Ruth chattered on. She would borrow a night-gown, her coat would serve as a dressing-jacket. She would be quite all right. He had better go to the ancestral hall, garage his car and arrange to spend the night there. He could send Mrs. Flack to make arrangements while he was away. Everything was settled, bar obtaining her a bedroom. That Ruth knew would be quite easy. Roy might ring the handbell out on the landing to summon the boy.

Ruth had forgotten her feelings of impatience for dull humanity, forgotten the prosperous women of the hotel lounge and her smart friends who had seen and read so much. Being with Roy acted on her like a tonic. She felt refreshed and alert, anxious to unravel the history of the Greyhound's occupants. These people, she felt, really lived; compared to them she was a dilettante. The effort of soft-natured townspeople to win a living from this rough northern village, Roy told her, was foredoomed to failure, possibly ruin. If the landlord was a sober, careful man instead of a loose drunkard, if his wife was a thrifty, hard-working woman, an existence might be forced from the reluctant village. As it was, three people expected to live on the Greyhound's profits, four if Clara was counted. According to Roy the thing was absurd; there was no hope for the present tenants of the Greyhound, less hope than a man in the condemned cell might have. That was why Tom looked tragic; he could foresee the end. Poor boy, Ruth felt a pang for him, though he was a fool to stay on the sinking ship. Why were people fools? Why could they not accept the obvious end of their dreams, before the crash came, and so escape the shock of catastrophe? The futility of Tom's hope, his anguished face, touched Ruth.

When he came up in answer to the bell's summons, Roy ordered coffee, "Could you find us a liqueur?" he demanded, "the last fine touch to this good meal?" Tom, pleased, told him, "Yes, sir, we have Benedictine and advocat." "Benedictine, I think," Roy observed, turning to Ruth. She nodded; the boy left quietly.

The book-case attracted Ruth; she went over to it. While more thrilling than the library of the hotel in Matlock, it did not promise much. There were several cheap reprints of books by Nat Gould, a thick volume of Wordsworth's poems, Young's *Night Thoughts*, *Green Mansions* by Hudson, and several books by popular living writers; most of them, she noticed, were detective stories. If she needed to read, Hudson, Wordsworth or Young would keep her splendid company.

She took a cigarette from Roy's extended case, then sat down by the glowing fire. So far her night's adventure was incredibly satisfying. Roy looked well. She smiled at him from her pleased thoughts. To-morrow she would see his home, the haunts of his youth.

The sensation they would create on their return to the Matlock hotel for lunch! She told Roy, so that he might laugh too.

IV

IVY had taken pride in preparing food for the Squire and his lady friend. When the coffee stood on the hob, ready to be strained, she made a pot of tea; Tom, she knew, would be glad of a cup. To-night his waiting knowledge was very useful. That the meal was a success the empty dishes he carried down bore witness. She set the coffee things on a tray, poured hot milk into a jug and strained the coffee. Tom came in with the half-bottle of Benedictine and two liqueur glasses. Both guests were full of praise for the dinner Ivy had sent up, Mr. Grovedon had suggested coffee and liqueurs would complete a perfect meal. Ivy smiled. Her insistence that a half-bottle of Benedictine should be stocked was fully justified now. When Tom had gone off upstairs with his tray, she drew two chairs close to the fire.

Tom was back; he accepted the cup of tea gratefully, murmuring, "Only another hour now, Ivy." She nodded. Their regular customers were beginning to wake up, from the increase of noise. At the moment she was more interested in the guests upstairs. She inquired: "What are they like to you, Tom?" Her brother smiled. "Very nice, Ivy, friendly without being familiar. The lady has not much to say, it's him that does the questioning. Wants to know little things about us and the house. I told him what I thought fit, and no more." "Good boy," Ivy nodded; "it doesn't do to tell everybody our business, does it? I should like to have a sight of her frock." "Very pretty." Tom described. "Coffee-coloured lace, but the coat, Ivy, it must have cost a hundred pounds." She had noticed the coat, and envied its owner for possessing it. "Who is she, d'yer think?" was her next question. Tom shook his head. "Hard to say. Only a friend, I should think. She calls him Roy, and he her Ruth. They are nice. I like 'em both." Ivy wished such guests came frequently; if they did things would soon improve at the Greyhound. People like that spent more in one night than a villager did in a month. Tom made out the bill on a sheet of paper, and added it up. It came to thirteen and six, counting in coffee and liqueurs. He showed it to Ivy, who shook her head over it, dubiously. "It seems an awful lot, Tom," she said. The boy's voice rose. "Don't be silly, Ivy, it's very reasonable; look at the items. If I charged double they might think we were a bit stiff, though I doubt if they'd mention it. Besides, you had to cook it specially, as well as cutting into Sunday's joint." Ivy listened. Tom knew best; he had the advantage of her there. At least they would make seven shillings clear profit on the meal, which had been a pleasure for both Tom and herself to prepare and serve.

Tom finished the tea, passing the cup over for Ivy to refill. "Hurry up, you old tea party," she scolded him. "What they're doing in the bar without you, goodness knows." The boy laughed. "All right, I'll be there in a jiffy," he said. "Mr. Grovedon gave me half a dollar." Ivy was very pleased at that. It was nice for the boy to earn a bit, he was so good about getting no wages. At any town public he could earn twenty bob a week, beside his keep and tips. He was a good lad; she knew her luck to have such a brother. The boy got up and went out whistling. She set to work to try to clear up the mess her unexpected cooking caused.

A tap came at the door. "Come in," she called. The young Squire came in. "My friend, Miss Dorme, is anxious to spend the night here. Could you put her up?"

"Oh, yes, sir," Ivy told him. "The bed is aired, it only needs to be made up." "Then perhaps you will slip up and tell Miss Dorme yourself. I am just going up to the Hall to make sleeping arrangements for myself. Tell Miss Dorme I will be back very quickly." Ivy was delighted; she scented a romance going on partly under her own roof. Hurrying up to the spare room, she tidied Freddy's things away, quickly remade the bed and fetched out towels and a clean table runner. It scarcely took her five minutes. Then she went along to the sitting-room and, tapping at the door, entered.

Ruth Dorme stood up, smiling. "I've set your room ready, Miss," said Ivy, responding to the smile. "Perhaps you would like to see it." "I should very much," Ruth agreed. The spare room was beautiful, Ruth decided, instantly. The furniture was of dark oak in severe lines, the bedstead was big and looked most comfortable. On the walls was a pale milk-grey paper; three narrow frames of black wood containing silhouettes were their only ornaments. The curtains and bedspread were of pale grey cretonne patterned with a formal design of bunched cornflowers. Narrow bedside carpets of a matching blue shade were on the dark wooden floor. By the bedside stood a tiny arm-chair upholstered in dark grey plush. Ruth turned to Ivy. "What an exquisite room," she said. "I wonder you are not afraid to trust strangers in it." Ivy smiled. "It depends on the strangers, Miss. If I don't much care for the look of them, my brother sleeps in here, and they have his room for the night." "Very wise of you, I think," commented Ruth. She held up her hands. "As you see, I have no luggage; would you lend me a nightgown and a few things of that sort?" "With pleasure," Ivy agreed.

They went back to the sitting-room. Mr. Grovedon

stood in front of the fire. "Everything settled?" he inquired genially. "Yes," Ruth said. "I have been promised a loan of all I require and have seen the room in which I am to sleep. It is delightful." The Squire turned to Ivy. "When you go downstairs I should be glad if you would ask Mrs. Tapin to come up and see me," he told her. "Very well, sir," she replied. "I expect she will be in the smoke-room by now."

She delivered the message to Mrs. Tapin, then returned to the kitchen. Everyone in the house would be talking of Squire's visit with the young lady. Now she knew what the coffee-coloured frock looked like, too. A nice young lady. Quite a lady in spite of all she knew folks would say, of that she felt sure. The Squire, too, she liked him. Most polite he was. The perfect gentleman. Grovelace folks might talk till they were blue in the face. She would believe no more of their tales about him and his wildness. It had been a long and tiring day, seemed an age since she got up from bed in the morning. Still, it would soon be closing time. Sunday was a blessing; a pity it did not come twice a week.

During Tom's frequent absences as waiter on the Squire in the upstairs room, Clara kept her mother well supplied with drinks. Each time Mrs. Tapin made a pretence of paying, but Clara always brought her shilling back unchanged.

Clara felt excited. She was able to arrange a meeting with Fred down the cellar after time. Fred was drinking pretty steadily. The dull service bar bored him; there was no fun in talking to Asa Tapin and the other solemn-faced crows. He wanted to be where the fun was. He should need to put his foot down on Ivy's schemes if they were going to keep her and Tom out of the business like this. He decided that ten minutes after the service bar was turned over to him. When Tom came back on duty he scowled at the boy. Between Ivy and her brother his night had been spoiled. Clara was as bad, a nagging little cat, that's what she was. The idea of young Grovedon bringing a girl to the Greyhound amused him. He knew what taking a tart to a lonely country pub for food implied; he had done the same thing himself many a time. Before they left he would like to have a look at the girl.

For the last half-hour the clamour in the tap-room grew steadily. They were having a high old time there. When he went along they greeted him with enthusiasm. A game of darts was in progress. He joined the play, flattered by everyone's invitation to take a hand. The lowest score out of ten tries bought the tap-room men a gallon of beer in a share-out. Most of the players were skilled by years of winter nights spent in play. Among themselves it was a real contest of skill. When Freddy joined the game, its result was a foregone conclusion. He could not see the dart board clearly and threw in wild hopes of luck. When his turn was over, people patted him on the back, demanding their beer. He fetched a gallon jug full from the bar and decided not to play any more darts. He was tired, a bit muzzy. If the tap-room lot wanted any more beer, someone else must serve them. He played a game of dominoes with Pike; the old man won, but that at any rate cost him nothing. When the men started to knock for more beer, Fred encouraged them. "That's right, lads," he shouted, "someone is sure to come if you keep it up long enough."

Ivy in the kitchen heard the din. Fred was engaged, she supposed bitterly, Clara and her brother really busy. "Naxi, Naxi," she called; the greyhound came from behind the counter in the service bar at her call.

"Good dog," Tom encouraged him. "Go to your Missis." Ivy stroked his head, calling him "Beauty." He followed her into the tap-room. Freddy, she saw, was busily engaged in a conversation with an unpleasant man named Barle. The drinks fetched, she served Brightman last. His hand took her behind the knee. "Naxi," she called. The dog answered like an arrow, but the dark Lightning met him before he got to her side. Instantly there was an uproar. Brightman still held her leg, so that she was balancing on one foot. She picked up his brimming pint pot, flinging the liquid straight into his face. Released, she dashed into the kitchen for a pepper pot. A ring was formed round the dogs by the men, her husband among them. She pushed them aside fiercely, sprinkling the fighting dogs with wild lavishness. The pepper stopped them quickly; unconscious of risk, Ivy seized Pertinax by his tail, lugging him clear, someone stopping the other dog in a like fashion. She dragged Naxi out into the kitchen and gave him a long drink. The dog crawled under the table and commenced to lick his wounds. Later she must bathe them. Old Tapin knew a lot about greyhounds; he would tell her what to do. Silly old Naxi, always in trouble, though he was a good sort to come so gallantly to her aid. She went out of the kitchen, shutting the door carefully behind her. Back in the tap-room she found Fred and Brightman quarrelling. Josh swore he would have the law on Ivy; she set her dog on his without provocation, then peppered the poor beast. Not content with that, he declared Lightning's tail was damaged by the wrench given it to pull him clear. He was in an ugly mood; for a little while Ivy feared the row would develop into a fight between the two men. She pushed her way into the centre of the crowd, and shook her fist in Brightman's face. "You get out of here," she told him angrily, "and don't come in again, because you won't be served if you do." He turned and went, the greyhound at his heels. Such an easy victory surprised her; she was pleased. Though they could not afford to lose a customer, they would be better for the lack of Josh. George Lowe of the Straycross Black Horse was welcome to him. She hoped that he would never put his foot inside her house again, so that it would save a row, for she was determined not to serve him any more. Tom and Clara must be told, and Freddy persuaded to accept her wish on this matter.

V

TO Roy's surprise Ruth's interest was maintained about the Greyhound people. She thought Tom should leave before the crash came. With work in London he could provide his sister with a temporary shelter when she needed one. Eventually he must leave the Greyhound; it would be best for him to go now; in staying till the end he must suffer unnecessary pain and humiliation. Inability to avert the crash would only add to his fruitless suffering.

Ruth went to the window; pulling back the curtain blind, she peered out. The night was dark, a few jewels of twinkling light hung suspended in the blackness. The night air was cool and fragrant, sweet from the rain.

Roy sat by the dying fire smoking; she turned to him, saying, "Soon I shall go to bed. I feel rather tired. You were a dear to bring me away from Matlock." "You will not get much quiet till about eleven," Roy warned her, seriously. "These people do most of their work before turning in. You are an extraordinary woman, Ruth. What's the good of worrying about these folk? You can't help them." Ruth stared at him.

"I might think of something in bed," she told him. "If you lend them money it would only prolong the agony, and you would never get it back," he said. Ruth laughed, saying, "I'm far too shrewd to do anything so foolish, Roy. Something of real benefit to them is what I am trying to think of." "What has made you take such a sudden violent interest in them?" he questioned.

"Boredom, I suppose, if I am honest about it. I like the boy and his sister. If I do nothing else I shall often think of them here, stuck up away in your unfriendly country."

Roy shook his head. "My dear girl, you can do nothing. Nothing at all. The case is hopeless from beginning to end. If their money holds out much longer they will be in trouble with the police. The house is badly conducted. Anyone can buy a drink at any hour of the day and night. The police hear things, you know. They are bound to investigate, then the landlord will forfeit his licence." "How do you know?" Ruth asked.

"Everybody in a ten-mile radius knows. You are foolish if you try and interfere. Ordinary people ought to be darn grateful for their ordinary lives."

"Don't preach, Roy, it does not become you." He laughed, though worried. "I wish you would put this idea out of your head, Ruth."

"Don't be silly, Roy," she implored. "Surely you can trust me not to do anything foolish."

"It is not that, Ruth. They will suspect your motives, try and discover some baseness in them. Or else they'll think you mad." "Perhaps I am a little," she laughed. "Well, you have amazed me, Ruth. You are a dear, you know, but don't you think your behaviour to-night is a little too impulsive? You know when I first met you at Marion Strangeways', I thought you were too clever to live. You are usually so calmly definite about life's happenings. To-night you make me feel both cynical and callous. But it's no go. I can't work up any agitation about these people. The man is the type that should have been born rich. His wife is too much in love with him to control him. The boy—well, I'm a bit doubtful about him. A little bit abnormal, I should think. They are in for a rough time, poor devils, and that's that."

Ruth listened closely. All Roy said was probably true. "Anyway," she promised him, "I'll sleep on the thought. Come to breakfast, and if I am still keen on doing something for these people we can discuss it then." "All right," Roy agreed, half relieved. Women were uncertain. In the morning she might have forgotten all about it.

He watched her, wondering if he proposed to her again now, she would take him. The queer events of the night, their unexpected meeting and adventure—would it influence her in his favour? He felt it would be trying to take an unfair advantage of her. The desire to ask her was very great. Before when he asked her she seemed unable to take his proposal seriously. Here, in this room the bond of their affection and sympathy gained strength. In spite of all her reputation for being clever, she seemed like a young girl who does not understand things. It was not that she was incapable, but that for the time her heart governed her brain, clouding its reason with a mist of pity.

Ruth's mind circled round in a vain repetition of

thought. The impulse to help the boy and his sister guided it. The boy was pathetic, his eyes wistful, his lips held in. She noticed the look of strain on his face. If it were true that he knew the inevitable end, how he must suffer, day by day, in that atmosphere of gradual ruin. The sooner the end came for him the better. The woman, she was the victim of her passion—retract her worship and she could be free. The landlord, whom she had not seen, he too could save himself by applying a dignified discipline to his way of life.

How simple.

So simple that these people on the brink of ruin must have thought it out for themselves. They must have done that much. All three of them, then, remained wilfully where they were. Roy had gained many good reports of the boy, the way he worked and struggled. Ruth saw it all in a flash. The situation told bluntly savoured of comedy rather than tragedy. The boy trying to help the landlady and her husband, the woman trying to save her man, the man refusing to help himself, remaining unhelpable; they too because of it.

A knock came at the door. It was Mrs. Tapin. When Ivy gave her the Squire's message she had not felt entirely sober, so she sat still till she felt a little more steady. A walk down the lane blew the mist from her brain; she felt ready for any questions now. She came in, a dumpy figure in dull black clothes. "Evening, Squire, sir." She bobbed her head. "'Evening, lady." She bobbed again. What a tale she would tell all over the village to-morrow!

VI

THE last hour came, bringing an increase of trade as it always did. People emptied their glasses hurriedly and called impatiently for more. It was as though life must come to an end when the doors of the public-house closed on them. As the time fled by people became more free, their tongues clacked excitedly, they spent money more freely, with greater generosity. By half-past nine the tap-room was deserted, its rowdy crowd having drifted into the smoke-room and the bar. The more sober type, dismayed by the increase of high spirits, left the house unwillingly, driven by their pride. No one ever knew what mischief might hatch out during the last precious minutes.

Tom and Ivy were both anxious and tired. The evening's experience had left Ivy shaken. First her quarrel with Freddy, then the coming of Squire Grovedon and the young lady, and finally Naxi's fight with Josh Brightman's dog and the trouble that ensued. She was frightened of Brightman. He was hard and determined; she hoped he would never find her alone in the house. Fred might laugh; he did not know Brightman. That he would keep away from the house was too much to expect.

Tom kept a watchful eye on the company. He did not want any "drunks" on the premises when "time" was called. Old Gaunter had a nasty habit of lingering about the Greyhound toward closing time. Clara came in with a tray of dirty glasses. "That Mr. Badge wants a drop of gin," she called. "All right," Tom answered, reaching down the bottle. Clara drew off a jug of beer, refilling the glasses. Pouring a measure of gin into a pony glass,

Tom put it on the tray. He whispered, "No more drink for Mrs. Hacks. She's had enough. She's almost tight now. Pass it along to the others." Clara looked quickly at the old woman. "All right," she nodded. "You'll have to watch her." "I will," replied Tom grimly. Clara was a good girl in the trade. In the right house she would be invaluable. Tom recognised that she was quick and smart, with a shrewd head on her.

Every seat in the small bar was occupied. People were leaning up against the counter. The room was blue with tobacco smoke; it was stuffy and reeked of spilt beer. Tom flung a fresh supply of dry sawdust in the counter box.

In the smoke-room Fanny Turl thumped away at the piano. Someone started to sing "Don't go down in the mine, daddy," other voices took the refrain up. Those who did not know the words hummed vigorously. All had realised the end was near now. Song after song they bawled mournfully. Only those songs that had maudlin words were honoured by an encore. . . . Most of them enjoyed the singing thoroughly. The false emotional appeal of such songs transformed their hearts for the time being. Tom listened in grim disgust. Most of his customers he knew were quite capable of going home and beating their wives when the orgy of sentimental sloppiness was over. He noted the songs contemptuously. "She's the kind of a girl that men forget." "Ring down the curtain." "Roses of Picardy." "And a little child shall lead them." They would come back to that when he called "time." People's appetite for intoxicating liquor never ceased to amaze him, while he was disgusted by them. His early life and environment taught him that such appetite provided his bread and butter, and that his business was to sell drink, not to worry about its effects on those who over-indulged in its fleeting delights. As a boy of sixteen he had once got drunk through carelessness, but the headache with which he awoke next morning and the thrashing he received from his angry, unsympathetic father, cured him of all trifling with intoxicants. He had not needed a second experience. How they had chaffed him about it at the Crown. To a customer's dig, "You couldn't stand last night, Tommy," his father put in grimly, "Ay, and to-night he can't sit." Everyone laughed at that; one wag asked, "Which hurt most, Tommy, head or arse?" He had flamed red, not answering. "Bit hard on the lad, aren't you?" someone suggested to his father. "The boy's head was not made to sit or stand on; it's for him to use, sensible like," the old man answered.

A man came in, pushing his way to the counter. He was stocky and fair, dressed in neat black clothes; he wore a white silk scarf twisted round his neck. He smiled at Tom. " 'Evening, Tom, 'evening all." " 'Evening, Alf," said the boy; the crowd echoing his greeting. "You're late; glad you won." Alf laughed. "So am I, that. Two goals to none. Hard got they were and all. Lads will be along soon. They're at the Black Horse, Straycross like, now. Have a drink? Mine's a half." "Thanks," Tom answered, serving the drinks. "Here's health." "Same to you," said Alf, taking a long draught from his jar.

Suddenly Tom saw Mrs. Hacks lifting a mug of beer to her lips. He leant right over the counter, seizing her wrist. "Oh, no, you don't, Ma," he said, forcing her wrist over so that the beer spilt in a stream to the counter box, her hand unclasped letting the jar fall with a crash. No one said anything. Tom looked round furiously. "Who gave her that?" he demanded in angry tones. No one answered him; they all looked guilty but

Asa. "Anyway, she's having no more in this house tonight," he finished. Mrs. Hacks turned on him; she was a tiny, blear-eyed woman, dressed in rusty black, a shawl over her head. "You great bully," she called him. "Why can't a poor woman have her bit of pleasure on a Saturday night?" Tom told her fiercely, "You shut up or out you go." The woman dabbed her eyes tearfully, "I'm only a poor old woman having me pleasure," she moaned. "You'll get no more pleasure here to-night," Tom assured her firmly. The woman turned. "I'll go. 'Night all." She leant against the counter, fumbling with her purse. "Just half a pint afore I go," her voice wheedled. The boy remained firm. "Not a spot," he said, shaking his head. Drawing herself upright, she cursed him viciously, "Blast you, may your teeth rot out." "That's enough from you," Tom told her. She subsided, grumbling, into a violent fit of hiccups. Tom was an old hand; it needed a smart customer to get a trick up on him. He knew all the dodges, knew the very depths to which people would go to obtain another drink. Business stayed brisk. Clara came to and fro from her room every few minutes. Tom could hear Fred's strident voice singing with the others. He would be glad when the clock told him ten.

Ivy came in from the passage. "How goes it, Tom?" she inquired. "All right. How's Fred? Tight?" was Tom's whispered question. "Nearly." Ivy's voice was weary; she passed a hand over her brow. "That row with Brightman did it. He drank two doubles straight off." Tom nodded; he knew. Freddy dealt with most situations in the same way. With him one drink led to another; endless others till he was too drunk to drink.

The rest of the football team came in. Ivy helped Tom serve them with beer. She washed glasses in quick haste, turning them upside down on the drainer; that was all the drying they were likely to get to-night. "What's wrong with Mrs. Hacks?" she wanted to know. "Drunk," Tom told her. "She drinks as much as they'll serve her with at the Black Horse, then she comes on here." Ivy agreed. "That's true." "Well, she's got some hopes," said her brother, emphatically. An ordering customer asked Ivy, "What'll you have, Missis?" "A port," Ivy thanked him. She turned to Tom. "I shall be glad when it's time." The man asked, "You, Tom, what'll you drink with me?" Tom drew half a pint, lifting it in acknowledgment. "Your health. How's the wife?" The man, old Pearson, an overseer at the pithead, grumbled, "Not too well. She's always on the worrit about things." Tom nodded his head sympathetically. Worry. That was the bane of his own existence. Yet he could not help worrying. If he was like Fred, it would be a poor look out for Ivy.

The singing came to an end. Soon they would begin all over again. Tom looked at the clock. It seemed to be moving too slowly. Funny the way Saturday night got on his nerves. He must brace up. No use getting on edge—none at all.

He wondered what Miss Dorme and the Squire would think of the noisy ballad singers. Not much, if they were anything like himself. The singing possessed little merit, and no beauty; words were dragged off in too long nasal sounds.

Still, all things considered, he was beginning to live in better understanding with the village. The qualities of determination and pluck possessed by its inhabitants were admirable. It was unfair to judge them on that count. Their Saturday night's pleasure—Widow Hack's term was apt. The singing was a herd movement, a mass urge to something they felt better than their daily existence. As a mass Tom disliked them, but many of them as individuals he liked very much. Young Alf Weater, the football captain, George Phips and old Ben Hepple, the shepherd, were fine men, magnificent of body, possessing rough nobility of mind. Tom sighed. Who was he to judge them? He could not have endured life as they led it. There was no merit in despising genuine hardship. The poverty of the country-folk seemed to him even more distressing than that of towns-people. It seemed the rule rather than the exception. There was not long to go now, he told Ivy; she nodded, smiling. She too would be glad when the last man was out and the place shut.

Tom looked at the clock. "Five minutes, gentlemen," he called. Everyone drank hastily, re-ordering. Tom and Ivy worked furiously. Knowing they had only a few minutes left gave them an increase of strength. Alf Weater got up. "'Night, Missis. 'Night, Tom. 'Night, all!" he said cheerfully, and was gone. Old Asa sat up, looking; he took a long drink from the glass jar. When "time" was called he would be ready. Saturday he drew his pension, so could afford an extra drink; that was the only good Saturday was. Sunday was a far better day. Folks behaved proper on a Sunday, neat and quiet, not bawling sloppy songs fit to deafen people. He looked round, frowning. Folks were not what they once were. The Greyhound either. Landlord made too free with the ragtag of all the three villages. No wonder the police kept an eye on the Greyhound. P.C. Gaunter would catch that Freddy out yet. Asa smiled sourly; he felt nothing but contempt for the landlord and his wife. The boy, Tom, was the only one he had any use for. He respected the lad.

Tom was on the go all the time. He kept the counter swabbed down and things tidy as far as was possible. Ivy looked at the clock; the last minutes dragged so, but it would soon be over. She sighed in thankful anticipation.

Clara came in through the door. She looked flushed and excited. "An advocat, eight whiskies and a double brandy, please, Tom," she ordered. Tom gazed at her, staggered. He had never served such an order all the time he had been at the Greyhound. Perhaps the Squire was standing a treat? He did not think so. It would have been a gallon of ale among the house's visitors. Not whisky, brandy or advocat. "Who for?" he asked, sharply. Clara put her head up. "The boss," she announced curtly. Tom was furious. "You tell him if he wants 'em to come and fetch 'em himself." Coming aggressively forward, Clara demanded, "Are you going to get them for me, or shall I help myself?" "You're not coming behind this counter," the boy informed her fiercely. "All right," said Clara, maliciously, "I'll fetch the boss, and tell him what you say." She flounced out. The crowd stared at Tom with interest. There would be some fun soon. "If only I were bigger," the boy wailed to Ivy, "he wouldn't come behind, either." "He's mad," Ivy declared. "How much would that lot cost?" She reckoned on her fingers. "Eight and two pence," the boy told her quickly, "and nothing in the till for it. How much beer he has given away already to-night goodness knows. He can't keep on, Ivy. No one could." Fred came in through the open doorway. The crowd round the counter drew back to let him pass. They watched curiously. "What the hell are you two playing at?" he blustered, fiercely. "Trying to make a fool of me?" "No need to try," countered Tom, with swift bluntness. Fred lifted his hand with a threatening gesture. "I'll give you a bash if you sauce me, my lad," he informed Tom. "You touch him, if you dare, you great oaf," Ivy shouted at him. Her pride was broken, she was down. "He threw a jug of water at me to-night, he did," she told the company.

Someone tittered. Coming to the door Clara watched, a cold smile on her face. Fred went behind the counter. "Get out of my way," he said, pushing roughly past Ivy. "You do nothing but whine. It's a pity if a chap can't have a bit of fun in his own house of a Saturday night." He started to get the drinks ready. Mrs. Hacks came to the counter. "A drop of gin, if you please, Mr. Flack, sir," she whined. "All right, Ma," said Fred, serving her. "You have that with me." "Can't you see she's drunk already?" interposed Tom, hoarsely. Fred took no notice of the boy. Mrs. Hacks swayed unsteadily on her feet. She leered round triumphantly. "Thank you, Mr. Flack, sir. Your very good health, sir. May you long be landlord of the Greyhound, sir." Someone in the smoke-room started banging for more drinks. Clara ignored the sound; she was too intent on watching the scene in the bar. The noise of clanging mugs, the forlorn chant of "And a little child shall lead them," became deafening. Tom looked at the clock. Not a whole minute left. He took a deep breath and shouted with all the power of his lungs, "Time, gentlemen, please. Time. Time." Ivy's voice took it up. "Time, please. Drink up!" In the smoke-room men were bawling for drinks. "Be quick," Clara called, impatiently. "Be quick." "Half a mo," answered Fred, pouring out his brandy. "It's time, Fred," Ivy reminded him. "I'm landlord here," he snapped, curtly, "and I'll do as I damn well please. Here you are, Clara," picking up the tray.

Someone came bolting up the passage with clattering feet. It was Alf back. "Tom," he called, excitedly, "the policeman's waiting round the corner. I just nipped back to warn you." He disappeared. Fred dropped the tray with a clatter. "Time," he shouted. "Time, gents. Good Lord! Time! Time! out you get. Time! Time!" He bundled them hastily out into the passage. Tom cleared everyone out of the smoke-room. "Time!" he called. "Haven't you got any homes? Time! Time!" He watched Freddy's frenzied efforts to clear everyone out with contempt. "Blasted fool," he said, coldly. Clara started to wash glasses, Ivy to wipe them. Tom fastened the back door and returned to the bar. Fred was there. He sat down heavily, mopping his forehead. "My God! that was a near go," he said. No one answered him.

PART THREE
THE HOUSE CLOSES

I

CLUTCHING the half-crown that the young Squire gave her, Mrs. Tapin went down the stairs softly. Telling the young Squire and his fancy piece all she wished to of the Greyhound folks had been pleasant. She wished she knew why they were so interested. There was something funny somewhere. Later, in pleasant solitude, with old Asa abed, she would think it out. If she had not smelt a scandal it would surprise her. In the smoke-room folks sang "And a little child shall lead them." Mrs. Tapin cackled with soft, grim laughter. There was no one about in the passage. The kitchen door answered quickly to her firm pressure. Only Naxi was there. The greyhound lay near the fire, licking his wounds with a tender, skilful tongue. The room was untidy and smelt of cooking, stacks of unwashed crockery littered the sideboard. For some minutes Mrs. Tapin searched, finding the clothes-line in the boot cupboard. She made a loose slip knot at one end. Going out into the yard she cast the line over a shelter supporting beam, with clumsy skill. Under the shelter stood a wooden table and two chairs. They were intended for the use of outdoor customers, but no one ever used them. The noose hung down over the table. From the kitchen window enough dull light came to aid Mrs. Tapin's design. She fastened the other end of the rope securely to a pipe, and then returned to the kitchen. For some moments Naxi refused the tempting morsel of meat she held near his nose. At last he made a snap, but she was too quick for him. "Outside, good dog," she coaxed. "Naxi." The dog followed her slowly on sullen feet. The hare smell drew him with fierce insistence. With clumsy effort he followed the smell on to the chair, then on to the table. He stood on the table, resting from pain, the meat hanging from his jaws. Without protest he allowed his enemy to slide the wide loop over his head. Using all her strength Mrs. Tapin pushed the table over. The dog struggled violently, its hind feet nearly touched the floor. Very quickly Mrs. Tapin fetched Ivy's little potato knife. It was very sharp and worn to a point. With it she stabbed the greyhound repeatedly till its struggles ceased.

After she had made the knife clean and put it back where she found it, she went into the smoke-room. They were still singing about the little child, so she knew they must be nearly drunk. In her pocket was the piece of meat that she had used to bait Naxi with; washed in a drop of vinegar water, it should serve Asa for his Sunday's dinner, and so not be wasted.

George Phips sat near the piano. "Hello, Ma," he called. She crossed over to him; he edged up making room on the form for her. When she was settled comfortably, she asked him greedily, "Buy me one." He laughed, shouting at the frowning barmaid, "Hi, Clara, your Ma wants a drink." The girl brought her a glass containing gin. Mrs. Tapin took it, and sipped it delicately. She nodded her thanks to George. The thought of the swinging bloody hound came to her as she followed Clara's deft movements. Clara would laugh.

Neat and swift, her haughty air an armour of defence, Clara moved about serving the customers. George eyed her woefully. She never looked his way save with disdain. It was all Flack's fault. If he had let Clara alone, George felt he might have stood a chance. Besides, it was not right. Flack was a married man. During a lull in the singing George started to sing loudly his favourite song. Others joined him, their voices moaning sadly. In the room above Ruth strove to catch the words. Some came, others eluded her.

> She's the kind of a girl that men forget . . .
> . . . a toy to enjoy for a while
> When a man settles down . . .
> . . . An old-fashioned girl . . . old-fashioned ways . . .
> Poor little . . . they call you a flirt . . .
> . . . here comes the bride, you'll be on one side . . .
> Just a girl that men forget . . .

Ruth laughed.

Clara was furious. She knew George sung it at her. Many of the others too. Ignorant swine. They made her sick. There was still a half-hour to go before time.

Mrs. Tapin sat in happy joy. The scandal of the young Squire and his flash piece would keep the village in gossip for the best part of a month. It was not often she got such a bit of luck. When folks knew that she had been sent for, many was the free half-pint she would get in exchange for a lurid description of the bad woman. It was a good thing the Flacks refused to put the young Squire up too. Grovelace village would not have stood such goings-on. If Master Roy wanted fancy women he had better seek elsewhere for a roof to shelter both. She was glad he did not take the brazen woman up to the Hall. Still, that was not much. Bad things often happened in parlours, and the Greyhound parlour, being upstairs, seemed much worse. Mrs. Creel, the cowkeeper, who supplied Grovelace with milk, came into the smoke room; she made her way straight over to Mrs. Tapin. The gamekeeper's wife greeted her with friendly joy. They did not like each other, though they often put their heads together for the furtherance of a tasty scandal. "See thee, George Phips," cried Mrs. Tapin, "here's Mrs. Creel, none-seated." George got to his feet shyly like an awkward bird. He gazed round self-consciously. Someone tittered; he moved over to the piano and stood there sheepishly nervous. Without a word of thanks Mrs. Creel flopped herself down in the place made for her; she breathed heavily. She was a tall, stout woman, with sandy hair tightened into a clumsy nest on the back of her head. Her face was specked with brown dots like a pear, her eyes were hard and pig-like. For a moment she sat still, her thin lips pursed primly. "Goings-on," she muttered gravely, "goings-on, as I never thought to sight." Mrs. Tapin waited. If Mrs. Creel knew a tale to tell, her own could wait. George had left his glass of stout on the table, his back was turned; she picked it up absently, sipped a little, retaining the glass in her hand. Mrs. Creel turned on her crossly. "Will thee tell me on Squire's besom or no?" she asked. Mrs. Tapin smiled. "I'll tell thee an' all. The woman's tall, like thee, none so big made like, see thee. A hussy, if ever I seen one. Her face raddled redder nor my hearthstone. Gold and jewels round her neck like a stall at wake. And a coat with fur tabs on. She stinks with pride, an eyesore to the humble." Mrs. Tapin was very pleased with her long description; she drank the rest of the stout. Mrs. Creel spoke softly. "Twenty years ago I set forth same words on your proud head. Stink with pride, that you did, Mary Anne."

"Aye," replied Mrs. Tapin, still more softly. "Made a young girl's mistake, I did that. A chance never came nigh you, Bess, did it?" Mrs. Creel was offended; she sniffed, then called to Clara. "A bottle of stout, me dear." Clara brought it quickly. "I'll have one too," said her mother, passing over her half-crown.

The knowledge that for to-night Mrs. Tapin was independent of even her daughter's position made Mrs. Creel forgive her quickly. There was a lot more she wanted to know yet. "How does young Squire behave with her?" "Passionate," declared Mrs. Tapin, vehemently. She was not going to tell Mrs. Creel the truth about the Greyhound's unusual guests; that was too dull to be worth retailing. Once she saw a thrilling picture at Chesterfield, all about forbidden love; she thought for a moment of describing a scene from it for Mrs. Creel's edification. That would not do, for the cowkeeper was a shrewd woman, with a doubting turn of mind. "I can't tell you any more," she told the woman. "It breaks my poor heart to think of such goings-on." When Mrs. Creel decided no more could be learnt she went out into the passage to let the gossiping women share her garnered information. She told them solemnly, "Behaving passionate, they were. Mary Anne Tapin seed 'em, with her two eyes." "Stuck-up piece of haughty tripe, if all done and said is true," put in Martha Sharman, the blacksmith's wife. "Her bumped into Josh Brightman and swore at he." "What did she say?" questioned Mrs. Creel, eagerly. "Sod you," Martha said in a shocked voice. She herself possessed a reputation for the use of strong language, but the strong words used by the Squire's new woman shocked her exceedingly. Mrs. Creel went back to tell Mrs. Tapin. "Don't fret thy fat; I knowed," the little woman assured her. Bess Creel hurried back to her friends, bitterly offended.

Mrs. Tapin joined in the singing; her thin, shrill voice lost in the volume of sound, she rocked backward and forward in an orgy of enjoyment. As fast as her glass became empty, Clara filled it again with rich black stout. Mrs. Tapin's voice grew shriller till it cracked, but she was too happy to mind.

II

FIVE minutes after the front door was shut, Tom heard Mr. Grovedon come down the stairs. He went out into the passage and unbarred the door. The young Squire set off down the lane at a smart pace after wishing the boy "good night." Tom kept the door open so that the light might serve to guide the Squire a little distance on his way. At last the sound of footsteps ceased. Tom sighed, and relocked the front door. The Squire seemed a nice sort of chap; the young lady was nice too. They had spent good money; that was Ivy's perquisite. She deserved it. They had praised the meal highly. He wondered again where he could have seen the lady, Miss Ruth Dorme; the name was not familiar, anyway. Perhaps it had been at the Bristol. That was the most likely place.

The bar was in a dreadful mess. In spite of all his mopping, the last few rush minutes always made a mess. Everyone was too busy to do anything but serve. In a methodical manner he set about putting things straight. Taking up the tray of spirits that Fred had just failed to give away, he sorted them out, pouring them back into stock.

The memory of Fred's face made him grin; he hoped his brother-in-law had learned a lesson at last, though he felt it was not likely. Freddy was a born mug.

Tom raked out the ashes from the tiny fireplace, wiped down the chairs and tables with his wet cloth. He sorted out the bottles, stacking the empties on one side of the bar, putting the full bottles back in their cases. He wound up the clock, opened the till, and collecting all the money he placed it in a linen bag. After supper he would count it up. In spite of business being brisk, they had not taken much money. Even the miners had not much to spend on drink these days. It took a lot of beer to put ten shillings in the till. Very few of the customers drank spirits or wine. Still, they had earned a bit extra with the Squire and his friend coming in. Ivy would get another five shillings for the use of her bedroom. Tom contrasted her charges with those of the Bristol, and smiled cynically; the difference was so great as to be absurd. The Bristol. . . . Tom sighed. Their takings for one day were more than the Greyhound took in a year.

When the floor was swept and the room roughly tidy, he turned down the lamp and carrying a case of empty bottles went out into the yard. The case was heavy. Unseeing he brushed into the hanging body of the dead greyhound. He dropped the case with a start of fear. At last, with faint courage, he put out a searching hand. The dog's body was warm; his fingers became smeared with congealed blood from the wounds on Naxi's breast. With an effort he went back into the house to find a knife and electric torch. For some minutes he leant against the ice-cold sink, faint from shock. Then he went back. With the sharp potato knife he hacked through the straining rope. The dog was quite dead, bloody and awful. Sadly he flashed a light on the carcase. He felt sick, horribly and violently sick; his body trembled. Desperately he regained control, remembering Ivy. Somebody would have to tell her. Somebody . . . he himself. He shuddered. Poor foolish Naxi. Who could have done it? Who had hated him? A thought came to him. Mrs. Tapin disliked the dog. So did Clara. She had been busy all evening. It was not her, then. Her mother? Tom put the idea out of his head; it was too foolish.

The old woman had not the strength. Carefully he lifted the heavy body on to a sack, then carried it into the wash-house. Getting a bowl of water, he bathed the wounded body, trying to make it less horrible. At last he gave it up; it was hopeless. If Ivy wished to see Naxi . . . Well, she must. With care he slid the dog into the old sack. Then he mopped up roughly all traces of blood in the yard. The dog's fearful struggles had spattered the whitewashed wall, the overturned table and chairs. He would tell Ivy later. She would not miss Naxi tonight, nor was she likely to come out into the yard. Poor Ivy. She would take it badly. It would hurt her soft heart, and frighten her by its omen of disaster. After her first grief, she would see in Naxi's terrible end foredoomed failure of all her plans for success. Tom wondered anxiously where he could hide the sack. The rats would get at it if he left it in the wash-house. Softly he stole back into the house. Ivy was not about. Clara and Fred, he supposed, were gone to bed. He looked in the smoke-room. Clara had set it tidy, ready for Sunday morning. Fred left the tap-room untouched. Tom sighed. If Fred stopped in bed next day he would have to get it shipshape. Fred was an idle swine. Just like him to clear off to bed, leaving his share of the work undone. Going to the cellar head, Tom paused. He could see a light. There was someone down there. Who? Fred . . . Fred . . . and Clara. Taking off his thin-soled slippers, Tom crept softly half-way down the stone steps. He could hear soft whispering voices. Freddy's and Clara's. To find Ivy and fetch her down was his first impulse. He abandoned it. She would soon find out for herself. For some time he had suspected them. Ivy suspected them herself now. It was only a question of time before she caught them out. If only she did not care for Fred. But she did. That was the whole crux of the matter. While Freddy kept that power, till Ivy's infatuation died, he could do nothing. He turned back, and fetching Naxi's body hid it in an old unused cupboard in the tap-room. That done, he washed his hands and sat down to supper. After a few mouthfuls he pushed the plate aside. He was not hungry. Naxi's mutilated body came swinging to his bruised mind. For a time he wondered, was he one of those unfortunate people who take trouble in their train wherever they go? Was he responsible for the misfortunes that overtook the Greyhound? Common sense came to his aid. It had nothing to do with himself, nothing whatever. By hard work and careful management Fred and Ivy could make a meagre living at the Greyhound. There should have been no Clara, no Mrs. Tapin, no Naxi, no himself. The fault was not his, but Fred's, Ivy's. With his money he could keep them going, tide them over till the summer came. Even with Fred's extravagance a couple of hundred pounds would do it. Tom considered his plan calmly. There were many reasons both for and against. Getting a scrap of paper and pencil, he made a list.

For	and	Against
For Ivy's sake.		For Ivy's sake.
For Fred's sake.		For my own sake.
Fred may have D.T.'s and die.		He might have 'em and live.
I can afford to.		The money will go after Ivy's.
I like being with Ivy.		
She is my sister.		Eventually she will have to come to me.
		Clara.
		Fred's gambling habits.
		A police raid.
		I dislike Fred.

SATURDAY NIGHT AT THE GREYHOUND

It did not comfort him much. For Ivy's sake they would be better out of the Greyhound. Away from a pub Fred would not be able to drink at all hours of the day and night. The question of Fred's morality affected him only in that it affected Ivy. It was her happiness that he sought. For Ivy Tom felt he could do things of incredible bravery. He would like to shield all ugliness from her eyes with his body. The thought of the pain she must yet suffer twisted his heart. The futility of his own efforts to protect her goaded him sharply. His love made her no armour. Naxi . . . Fred and Clara. . . . There was that for her to know and accept. . . . To know and accept, to lie awake night after night and think on. And he could do nothing to fend off the blows that were to fall on her. . . . Conscious of Ivy's faults, she still remained to Tom a creature of beauty. His thoughts dwelt on her always with tender possessive affection. That she was his sister seemed in itself a miracle. The feeling he had for her was sunk too deep in his memory for him to desire to analyse it. She was lovely, tender and sweet. She came and took the love he offered graciously; he knew unwillingly that she was not conscious of its depths. To suffer in her stead was his constant aim. Though he seldom achieved this, to do so gave him emotional happiness. To him her welfare was his religion. His thoughts swung back to the Greyhound. Keep it going? Let it fail? He could not decide. Left to Ivy, she would choose to keep on. Ought he to protect her from herself, from her own desires? The time had not yet come. Wait till it did. . . . Then he would have to decide. If Ivy approached him, pleading. . . . That night when both she and Fred had drunk too much, the swine shut her out. Locked her out of her own bedroom. A chance visitor occupied the spare room. It was to him

Ivy had come, weeping, her slender body cold and trembling. With gentle hands he touched her, soothing her to sleep, her head on his breast, the fragrance of her hair in his nostrils. He had dreamt, lying awake. She was his own child. A child of joy and beauty. Above all things in the world he loved her, loved her with fine tenderness. Desiring no return but the consciousness of her presence. . . . Very gently he tried to get out of the bed, so that she might have greater comfort. In sleep she clutched him, and he heard the whisper from her lips, "Freddy!" He lay very still. The grey dawn slid slowly up, re-establishing forgotten things. Tom dared not move, for his sister still slept. When she awoke at last in troubled shame and confusion it was he who restored and gave her comfort out of his love. To whom else could she have gone? he asked tenderly. Her coming proved she knew of his love. What had pride or shame to do with that? Love was too great a thing. That night, in spite of its misery for Ivy, was for Tom a precious thing, a treasure of memory.

Tom hoped to see Spring's magic awake the woods to beauty. He thought of bluebell flowers massed in fragrant loveliness, to see the sun peer down through the soft green of young leaves; hedgerows gay with primroses, where violets nestled to reward the searcher, and the tiny star flower of the barren strawberry when the air would be soft, sweet from the light and fragrant rain. He would want to go out, bare-headed, into the rain. The thought gave him a moment's fleeting joy. After the shower the sun would come out, the land would be all beauty. Spring was hope awake and refreshed. Life would seem more kind because of the beauty. If he were there to see, if he were there to see. . . Tom made no profession of religion. In the old days neither he nor

Ivy had had to go to church or Sunday school. He wished to have life wholly in harmony, without ugliness —that was, he realised, an impossible dream. Even his own share towards that gracious state was seldom done. The jealousy with which he regarded Fred was not conducive to happiness or content. The ugly things stayed ugly; trying to ignore them did not vanish them away. If he tried hard he might influence Fred. He knew the thought was but a false hope, so Ivy deceived herself. No one could alter Fred; the change must come from within.

Tom heard his sister coming down the stairs. His heart-beats quickened painfully. Ivy must not see anything wrong with him. She was so quick to sense things. He drew the money softly out of the dirty linen bag, then commenced to add it up swiftly.

It had been a poor night in spite of all the last hour's rush.

III

OUTSIDE the door of the guest-room Ivy paused to light her candle. She travelled down the steep stairs quickly; her short talk with Miss Dorme had been pleasant. To have such a distinguished guest beneath her roof was exciting and a happy forecast of prosperity to come. She was both thrilled and pleased. Such a visitor justified her disposal of the good furniture belonging to her mother. Miss Dorme gratefully borrowed her best night-gown, a brush and comb and various oddments necessary for making her toilet. Ivy felt very gratified in possessing such nice things to lend. That was one thing about Freddy: when he bought anything for her it was always nice, good quality. The night-gown was one of her most treasured things, a soft, filmy garment of unstarched lawn. Someone had embroidered roses in delicate tinted cottons round the neck and on the short sleeves. Freddy had taste, and when he had any money he liked to buy her pretty things, little costly trifles that she felt were too extravagant to get herself. He was a darling, though foolish. Most men were. Even Tom a little. How happy they could make her, her two big boys. Her heart was warm to them both; she loved them dearly. She must try hard to be a little more tolerant of Freddy's impulsive ways. Tom must try, too. Going into the kitchen she found Tom sitting at the table. He had a piece of paper and was making up the night's takings. Putting her gentle hand on his shoulder she leant forward to see the total. Tom's hand came up to hold hers in place. There was something wrong Ivy knew at once. Tom always betrayed himself by an infrequent gesture of tenderness. All her happiness went at his touch. Her heart started to thump. She must remain calm. She felt suddenly tired, very tired and weary. She drew her hand away from Tom's clasp and sat down heavily.

The kitchen was an untidy, miserable place, she thought. Soon the dull fire would be out. Lamplight gave a desolate dim reality to things. She did not like it, it depressed her. Tom wore a grim look on his face. She hated to see it there. Presently, she knew, he would start to complain of Freddy. Pulling out a packet of cigarettes he offered them to her; she took one, he too. When they were lit, he scooped up the loose money, putting it in the linen bag. He grunted with disgust: "Three pounds odd." Ivy nodded; she wondered aloud, "How we'll keep going I don't know." "Nor me, either," said her brother, crossly. "Why, I'll bet Fred's given a quid's worth of drink away to-night while we were busy with the Squire." All Ivy's resentment against her husband awoke. She remembered the jug he had thrown at her.

Bitterly she commented, "He's mad." "Yes," agreed Tom. "He changed his tune pretty quickly when he heard the cop was outside, didn't he? Funny, that was." The boy laughed shortly. Ivy smoothed out the folds of her black skirt. She spoke with slow bitterness. "The fool. It's a wonder we've not been caught before now." All the suffering she had endured since her marriage came up. She knew there was more to learn. Tom knew even now. She did not want to know any more; at last she was nearing the end of her tether. She would like to escape in blind ignorance of the new secret Tom held. "I've a good mind to take everything I can lay my hands on and clear out," she told Tom fiercely. The boy nodded eagerly. "I would if I were you. Why don't you, Ivy? You'd get a barmaid's job anywhere, easy." She answered him sadly, "I'm a fool, Tom. I talk too much. I couldn't leave him. He'd be in the gutter in less than a month." Her relapse into sadness hurt Tom. Surely she must see the way in which she too was heading. With brutal earnestness he assured her: "You'll be in the gutter with him too, if you stop. He'll never alter. He'll never be any good to you as long as he lives." Ivy knew, but false hope led her on. "If only he'd try," she said. "I don't grudge him a drink. If only he'd keep sober and not give the stuff away." Tom lit another cigarette. He told Ivy solemnly, "He is past curing. He never was any good. He never will be any good. Sooner or later you'll have to leave him. Poor Dad would turn in his grave if he could see us now, Ivy." Ivy shuddered. "He would that," she commented. "Me in the business all my life, as you might say, to come to this. I wish we'd never come here, Tommy. I'm frightened. He's that lazy. Still, there is nothing I can tell you that you don't know about him." That was true enough, Tom felt. "The tap-room has not been touched," he informed her. "The reason Fred and I don't get on very well together is because I know all about him. When he's coming out of one of his soft drunks he tells me all about things. Slobbers it all out." He mocked in imitation of Fred's voice: "Never loved another woman, Tommy, lad. The one I love, she hates me." "I don't," said Ivy, her lips white, the tears hovering in her eyes. "I wish you did. Oh, how I wish you did," came from Tom. He eyed his sister, anxiously. The strain was beginning to tell on her; she looked tired and ill. Quietly she said, "I wish I did hate him. I wish I did. I could lower myself to do the dirty on him then."

The boy thumped the table violently, the money-bag clinked and the lamplight jumped and flickered. His voice was hard and cruel. "I'd like to give him a darn good hiding, I would." Then he softened, asking tenderly, "Why didn't you take Arthur Wilkins? He did want you."

Ivy's voice was pathetic. "Fred was so lovely, I thought he'd change for me, Tom." The boy became scornful. "Change! Change! Hell! He'll not change till he's rotting in his coffin." The waiting tears rolled swiftly down Ivy's face. She shuddered. "Don't talk so dreadful," she gasped, her voice wailing. "You give me the creeps. Ugh!" Tom was tender in an instant. He patted her bowed head clumsily. "Don't cry, dear," he beseeched. "I'll not leave you. Saturday always makes me blue." Ivy lifted her head, patting her eyes dry. She looked round, then asked, "Where's Naxi?" Tom's heart beat painfully. It was coming. He managed to answer calmly, "I've bathed him, and put him in the tap-room." An idea took him. "Have a drink, old girl? It will cheer you up. The till owes me a couple." Ivy smiled. It was just like Tom. To please him she inquired: "What'll we have?" The boy got to his feet briskly. "You have a bottle of stout, I'll have a spot of port." "All right," Ivy agreed. "You'll hide the till money, won't you?" "Right oh!" he called, disappearing through the door. Ivy thought of him fondly. He was such a good lad. Only drank water during hours. If only Freddy would have done the same. But he never would. It was idle to have such a vain hope. All her visions and hopes, were they equally vain? She hated to face the truth; she pushed the question from her thoughts.

Presently Tom returned, carrying a tray. He drew the cork from the stout bottle and poured the smoky liquid out skilfully. He lifted his own glass, handed Ivy hers, exclaiming cheerfully, "Cheerio, old girl." Ivy lifted the glass to her lips, then put it down without drinking. She stood quite still, her head on one side, listening. Tom stared at her fearfully. Sharply she demanded, "Where's Clara?" The boy answered swiftly, "Gone to bed. Where else should she be?" Ivy stared at him doubtfully. "Fred's not in our room. I'll just nip up to Clara's room and see." She lit the candle hastily and went upstairs. Clara's room was empty, her bed untouched. Ivy fled into her own room. Fred was not there.

Tom waited for her impatiently by the kitchen door. Fred and Clara were still down the cellar, he thought. He had not heard them come up. Ivy came running down the stairs. She rushed into the room, talking wildly. "They're not upstairs, either of them. I must find him, Tom, I must find him. She is trying to take him from me." Sick at heart Tom said bluntly, "Let her have him. He's not worth keeping." Ivy looked at him fiercely. "He's mine," she declared vehemently. "Mine. She shan't have him."

In a cold voice the boy told her deliberately, "She's got him. They're both down the cellar." Ivy's brain hurt. "What?" she demanded, then more fiercely, "I'll kill her. I'll kill them both." Tom took her in his arms, holding her tight. "Steady," he warned. Ivy broke from him. "Be quick," she moaned. "I must be quick." She went to the cellar head.

Fred heard her coming. His grip on Clara tightened. He put his mouth down to Clara's. For a moment the girl struggled in wild, unreasoning fear. Then she kissed him with the added ardour of her thoughts. In spite of soppy Ivy, Fred was hers. He was going to let Ivy see them, instead of pretending that he and she were engaged in some legitimate business down the cellar. Her heart was wild with triumph. Ivy would see.

Holding the candle above her head, Ivy came in. Fred gulped under her gaze. Defiantly he kissed Clara's white neck. For a moment the three of them were like statues. Clara got nervous. Why did not someone speak? She felt Ivy's eyes piercing her back. She released herself from Fred, and faced her enemy brazenly, demanding haughtily, "Well?" Ivy's voice came sobbing, "Fred." The barmaid turned to him. He said nothing. "Say something, Fred," she urged. His remark when it came amazed her. "Better get upstairs. My feet are cold," he said, leading the way out of the cellar. Clara followed him closely. She wondered what was wrong with him. Why had he held her like that if he had not meant Ivy to see how much he cared? Ivy followed at her heels, storming fiercely now.

Tom stood in the middle of the room. "The swine," he thought bitterly. Poor Ivy. Clara marched in, her head high; she stood by the table. Ivy followed, and Fred brought up the rear, a foolish grin on his face. Ivy stormed, her voice shrill. "You hussy. You slut. I've a good mind to turn you out now. You slut. You'll go first thing in the morning." "I shan't go far," answered Clara, insolently. She turned to Fred. "You'll come and see me, won't you?" His grin vanished. "No," he answered, shortly, speaking to them all. "I'm sick of the lot of you. You can go to hell for all I care." Ivy wrung her hands. "Hell," she whimpered, "that's true. Hell!" Tom stared at her. Would she never break under Fred's cruelty? If only her love would snap. He listened to Clara's voice asking, "You love me, Fred, don't you? Don't let her upset you. You remember what I told you." She was anxious from fear. What sort of game was he up to? What did he intend to do? She repeated eagerly, "You remember, don't you, Fred?" Ivy turned on her husband fiercely, "What's that?" she questioned. "What have you to remember, Fred?" "Tell her, Fred," Clara urged, her voice impatient. "Yes, tell me, Fred," from Ivy. "God knows I have done my best for you." With unsuppressed triumph Clara faced her.

"I'm going to do something for him that you'll never do. Tell her, Fred. Don't turn on me now."

"Something you'll never do," she echoed to Ivy. "You liar," Ivy said swiftly. With disgust Clara turned on Fred. "You great coward," she said scornfully, then to Ivy, "I'm in the family way."

For a moment Ivy stared unbelievingly at the girl. There was no mistake. Why had not she seen it before? "My God!" she said softly. "My God!"

Not content with spoiling her life, he had spoilt

Clara's. She felt numb and sick. Clara stared round at them all, her face hard and sharp, then she walked out of the room, her head in the air.

Tom watched her go: he was bewildered by the turn of events. What could he do? Surely there was something. Poor Clara. Her brazen courage made her more pitiful to his mind. She was only a child. Poor kid. She would have a lot to bear through gaining Fred's affection.

Fred had taken off his shoes; he held his feet to the dead but still warm ashes. What a fuss folks made. He got fed to the teeth with them. It was too late to fuss when the damage was done. Clara was a smart girl. She never ought to have got that way. It was up to her now. Better send old Mrs. Tapin a bottle of gin and a quid note. She was no fool. It would not pay them to play tricks on him. They would not try. Waiting down the cellar with Clara had been a cold game. It had been worth it, though.

He glanced over at Ivy; she was weeping softly, her face held against Tom's chest. The boy looked hard and grim. He was a nasty little devil. Ivy would get over it, like she'd got over the other things. Perhaps he had been a bit of a swine. Still, it was all Clara's fault. Ivy would believe that. She would believe that. Believe him in spite of all her smug little prig of a brother said. Ivy loved him. She was not a bad sort. If he kept up an appearance of injured dignity, more sinned against than sinning, she would soon be round, anxious to forgive him, to accept his version of Clara's trouble. Tom would have to get out. The boy put his back up. Ivy was very different before he came, poking his nose round. He knew too much.

Fred saw Ivy's glass of stout, "Pity to waste it," he said to himself. The others took no notice. Tom's face looked proud. Taking the glass, Freddy emptied it at one long draught. He wanted them to go to bed badly. To his delight Tom moved. "Come along, Ivy," he said, "you'll be best in bed, my dear." Like a child Ivy obeyed him, clinging closely to his arm. She seemed blind. Tom led her upstairs gently.

As soon as Fred heard the bedroom door close he went to the service bar and had three large brandies in quick succession. Then he felt better. Up in the bedroom, Tom unbound Ivy's hair. He was like a mother with a delicate, sensitive child. If Ivy wanted to talk, well, she would, but that in her own time. He took off her jumper. She was like a tired baby, neither helping nor resisting. Very gently he urged her arms into the sleeves of a dressing-jacket. What would Miss Dorme think of their affairs if she knew? How absurd thoughts were! What did it matter what she thought? She was never likely to know. With long caressing strokes he brushed Ivy's hair. She loved him to do that. It was like a narcotic to her; the long regular sweeps that freed her mind from thought. She sat forward in the straight-backed chair, her eyes closed, a line of pain on her brow. Every time the brush passed it took her head back with a pleasant jerk. Like floating out into unconscious space. But she always came back. The damn clock started to talk. It often did. Freddy bought it for her in Birmingham a long time ago. Years and years and years ago. She could hear what it said quite plainly. "Freddy Clara, Freddy Clara." It would say it all night. Never stopping. Never stopping. Telling her what she knew. What she knew. Abruptly she turned her head from the kind brush. "Do you hear what it says?" she demanded of Tom, pointing to the clock. He shook his head. "No." Any fool could hear. "Freddy Clara." Her voice rose to a shriek. "Freddy Clara"; without a pause, "Freddy Clara." She broke down again, crying wildly, "What shall I do? What shall I do?" In dumb anguish Tom stood by. Only she could answer that; he could do nothing. It was horrible to be so barren of help; to fail Ivy when she needed him most. Thoughts of violent rage against Fred were unfruitful efforts; they only hurt him, made him ache with futile anger. People, Ivy, Clara, Freddy, himself had to work things out by experience, sadly gained. The life and death of millions touched them not. Experience was the only guide, individual experience; even that could be brushed wilfully aside, its lesson ignored or flouted. Ivy flouted it and so suffered, not once but time and time again. Her faithful, eager heart would perish loving Fred. Would Clara learn from the bitterness of her experience? Tom hoped she might. The price she must pay was high enough. Freddy learn? Tom's mouth set in its grim line. Freddy would never learn anything that he did not wish to. Neither would Ivy. The length of human endurance amazed him. Was Ivy's love so precious that she could sacrifice all else on the altar of it? Her pride, her ambition, her youth, her money. It seemed so, for willingly she had offered all that she had.

IV

UP in the bedroom Clara's boldness went from her. She felt like a naughty weak child whose misdeed had been punished with fiendish injustice. Ivy's treatment of herself was fair enough. In Ivy's place she would have done the same thing. It was Fred's callous indifference to her that rankled. The pride in which she held her conquest of him was utterly shattered, and at last she saw that from the very beginning his had been the conquest. Now he had dropped her. Ivy too. Unlike the wife, she was forced to accept dismissal.

What was she to do? It would be easy enough to get a paternity order against Fred. A few miserable shillings a week that would scarcely support the child he had saddled her with. All her dreams of success were ended. The future, a weary vista of long years in the dull village that she hated. An eternity of loneliness. The people whom she hated and despised would be able to have their revenge. They would take it, destroying her with their contempt. The beast whom her mother had married, how he would gloat over her downfall. People would never cease to gossip and sneer; the thought of them made her wince. As long as life lasted they would remember it against her.

In Chesterfield market-place the gossips would snigger as they told of her plight, the miners and their wives in Scrutton would laugh as they recounted her fall.

Fred.

He would escape all that.

People would wink and say, "Landlord at Greyhound is quick at wenching." Because he had brought her low, they would like him. He would laugh boldly, and the careful women would keep out of his way. By her loss of carefully preserved virtue she had put a glamour on him. No one minded a loose man, but such a woman, for her they had not even pity.

The image of Fred arose in her aching mind. She saw his fair skin, the gold of his hair as it lay on her young breast. Tears slid down her face and fell on to the bed. She heard again his whispers, the tender things he had said. And now, that was over. Over . . . everything but the pain of childbirth was over for her. But for him, he had everything. Ivy was upset more by hearing he would father Clara's child than by his lapse from faithfulness. And Tom, he had ceased to matter. He was merely one of the crowd who could discuss her trouble; he would blame her, as they all would. Even the virtuous would discover excuse for Fred.

The slow events of the long evening filtered through her brain. The scratch Fred's brooch had made showed red across her throat. It had been an evil omen. It was no use, she had known it as a sign of ill-luck. The little charm book told: "A prick from a pin before starting on an errand means bad fortune." Old Bedelia Gee knew her trouble instantly, and her inquiries and fumblings proved the truth of Clara's worst fears. Paying the old crone the half-crown she demanded, she fled back to the Greyhound, a sick feeling at the pit of her stomach. After a brief rest on her bed, she went down determined to have a reckoning with Fred. Tom's remark almost betrayed her to them then; she was so overwrought. Then Fred had dodged her, quite easily because of it being a Saturday night. At last she got him alone; her insistence brought about the meeting in the cellar after time. A tremor shook her violently. Suddenly she knew he kept her down there, dallying with tame embraces, till Ivy should come. Twice, then, he had betrayed her, twice; the second time was despicable, utterly cruel and unfeeling. Compared with Fred's treatment of herself, the dead Squire had behaved decently to her mother. The scorn with which she thought of that betrayal was nothing to the scorn she felt for her own. Her mother achieved the state which she sought. Compared with that success Clara's own affair proved an utter failure.

The fact that her own fate could not be altered was too terrible to face calmly. Lurid ideas flooded her brain; she might murder Fred, cut his throat as he slept. That done, go to the rustling stream and lean forward to meet its icy embrace. Then she would not see the talking women staring scornfully as she passed, would not hear their mocking voices following her along the lanes, would not be there for them to tear. Outside the churchyard walls at Straycross, deep in the red clay her spoilt body would moulder untouched by village gossip. She would have given them something extra to talk about. For hundreds of years they would keep her black memory in the Greyhound bar. Clara Tapin, Squire Grovedon's love daughter, who killed the father of her unborn child. They, the countless generations of Grovelace folks, would pause and wonder by the rough mound of her grave.

That was all a picture.

She would neither kill Fred nor herself. He was not worth it. Too soon Death might come for her, as it was. Who knew what would happen? She had yet to taste the waiting contempt of her mother's neighbours, and the pangs of labour.

The Grovedons, when they met her in the street, would they nod, or merely stare in cold disdain? Nothing they did could alter facts; she was of them, and they knew it. Roy Grovedon and his fine lady, did they think folks fools? He had been alone with the woman long enough for the worst to happen. Fancy a richly dressed woman like that allowing him to leave her at the Greyhound while he slept up at the Hall. All men were beasts. Folks said he fancied Rosie Marple, the still-room maid. Perhaps he did, and that was why he did not wish the two women to have a chance of meeting. What was the use of thinking about other people's troubles? She had more than enough of her own. The way in which Fred held her down the cellar, her back to the dim stairs, so that she could not see. Till Ivy was on them he did not let her go. And then he said no word, made no defence for her. Her threats and pleadings did not touch him. Ivy received the wounds. Poor Ivy, soppy Ivy; she and Ivy made a nice pair of hens for the lordly Fred. Hen-like she and Ivy had both pecked viciously, hurting themselves, not him, the cause of their strife. His vanity and complacency exceeded her own by far. The cool way in which he listened to her news, as though it had nothing to do with him.

If ever she got clear of the mess she was in, she would play safe in the future. The lesson Fred taught her on the practice of selfishness would never be forgotten. In the future she would only consider herself. It would be a clever man who made her his victim the next time. To think that she had been such a fool; in spite of all her proud resolutions she had fallen for the first attractive man who came her way. Such thoughts were galling in the extreme.

She got up from the bed, and by the light of a flickering candle washed the dirty tear-stains from her cheeks. Sooner or later her mother must know. Better go down to the cottage and get it over. Her mother might think of something, some way to get back on Fred, make him suffer a little of what she must go through. The cracked mirror made her look ghastly. Opening the door, she crept on stockinged feet past Ivy's room, and down the stairs. A thin line of light passed in from under the smoke-room door, cutting the darkness like a sword. Clara understood. Fred was there, drinking with some of his low friends. Showed how much her news upset him. Hatred engulfed Clara as she fled down the quiet lane. With all her mind she cursed Fred. Nothing could happen to him that would be bad enough. The dark hedge shadows passed unnoticed. Clara's inward eye saw Fred's body horribly mangled and bleeding, a fate that she hoped would overtake him.

When she reached the cottage she found the side-door locked. Anxious not to disturb Asa, she tried the window gently. From inside came a sound of someone moving. Clara expected her mother was rousing from sleep. With her fingers she kept up a low clatter on the window-pane. She heard the bar being gently raised.

Mrs. Tapin was frightened. Wakened out of her doze, she remembered the swinging greyhound. Had they found out that she had done it? "What's matter, girl?" she asked, lighting a candle with trembling fingers. Clara did not answer. Mrs. Tapin shivered; they must have found out. The suspense was awful. Why did not Clara answer her? She spoke again, asking sharply, "Have they found out, girl?" Clara's eyes widened, she stared at her mother in surprise, and answered quietly: "Yes." With a wail Mrs. Tapin picked up the hem of her apron and threw it over her head. She rocked backwards and forwards in terror. What would they do to her? They might send her to prison, even. People made so much fuss over animals these days. They would say, too, that Naxi was valuable. Landlord paid five pounds for a right dog. Clara watched her sway in the old chair. Sitting there moaning would do no good. Why had she not said something before, anyway?

Clara went over to the chair, snatching the apron from her mother's head. She shook her roughly. "Well," she asked, coldly, "what am I going to do?" Mrs. Tapin stared hard at her daughter, then she knew. She stood up, shaking with anger and relief. "Naughty slut," she screamed shrilly, "setting shame on us." Clara listened for a few minutes in silence, then seized by resentment she snarled fiercely, "Shut up, you'll wake dad, you old fool." A hoarse chuckle came from above. Old Asa stood on the top stair, grinning down at them. "Abominable harlots," he called, loudly. Glad to have a fresh object for her rage, Mary Anne Tapin snatched the alarm-clock off the mantelpiece and hurled it with all her force at the white-clad figure of her husband. It found a mark on Asa's body, for he gave a shrill yelp of pain, and the clock thudded back on the floor. Mrs. Tapin enjoyed an occasional fit of temper, for it kept fear in Asa, and relieved her own feelings. Every article in the room that possessed no great value in her estimation was hurled forcefully at the closed door of her husband's bedroom. Every filthy name she could remember she screamed too. Clara waited patiently. When the fit was over her mother would be easy to deal with.

The two women sat close to the tiny fire; a bottle of stout stood warming on the hob. When it was ready Clara fetched two glasses, filling one for her mother and pouring a little in her own glass. She tasted it delicately; her nose wrinkled at the bitter flavour. Mrs. Tapin smiled sourly as Clara shuddered: the girl would have other more unpleasant things to drink before she was through. Clara finished the stout with a quick gulp; wiping her mouth, she leaned forward and commenced to tell her story. Her voice was dull and thick. Mrs. Tapin sat up stiff as a bolt to listen, her head on one side. "Never thought of him in that way," she began, and her mother's head nodded decidedly. "Saw him in market-place, Chesterfield, on me day off. Didn't happen then, but next time. Went to see Bedelia Gee. I've clicked all right. That swine. He don't care twopence. Soppy Ivy told me to clear out. He won't do anything for me. He has finished with me; he said so. The swine. He's there now, drinking in smoke-room with some Scrutton lads."

Mrs. Tapin wept. Clara's downfall was different to her own. The girl's chance with the young Squire was never likely to happen now. No husband, no marriage lines. Nothing but a few shillings a week for the child was all Clara could hope for.

Mrs. Tapin's rage became directed against Flack. She emptied her glass, and gazed at Clara.

The girl sat very still, her face white and set. Mrs. Tapin started a tirade against Fred. She called him every evil name she could think of. Clara looked up, her face set hard, "Shut up, Ma," she said, "that don't help me."

Flack had got her girl in trouble, the thing was to get him in trouble too. Such trouble as he would not shake off like he had shaken Clara. Young George Phips, he, Mrs. Tapin thought, would be glad of a chance to prove his affection for Clara; he would give Flack a thorough hiding. That would not do Clara much good either. It would only add to the scandal. "George Phips would marry you, Clara," she ventured. "If he was the last alive he'd none get me," the girl told her bitterly. "I'm sick of men. I'll take no one yet."

The old woman sighed. Clara had always been an obstinate one. She did as she chose, and never would be said, not even as a little girl. Now she was in trouble. Nothing could be done. Mrs. Tapin's head ached; what a finish to such a good night. The drink she got free, and the half-crown from Squire, the bit of meat for Asa's dinner, then the end, Clara's trouble.

Going to the cupboard she fetched out a packet of woodbines. Clara refused one. Lighting her own, she smoked it thoughtfully. At last an idea came, the best of all. She jumped up excitedly. "Get your hat and coat on, quick," she commanded Clara. The girl got up slowly. The one word "Gaunter" from her mother galvanised her into action. In less than a minute she was outside, hurrying in the direction of Straycross village, where a few lights still hung in the dark of the night.

V

AT last the house was silent and still. Fred grinned as he moved round the smoke-room cautiously. He was not sober, though his brain worked in jerky movements. He worked slowly, with the unsteady determination of his mood. The fire had burnt down and the hanging lamp gave a good light. Drawn close to the big table was a small one. On it Fred placed bottles of spirits, glasses, cigarettes. He went into the service bar and getting down on his hands and knees he searched till he found Tom's loose board. He took the money and the scrap of paper, laughing softly at his own cleverness. It would be safe to let the boys in now, he decided. Opening the side-door, he sprayed the darkness with quick flashes from an electric torch. Soon came footsteps in answer to his signals. He held the door half-open so that his visitors might pass in. Closing the door softly he followed the men into the smoke-room; there were three of them and they worked in the Scrutton mines. Fred seized a whisky bottle and poured out lavish drinks for everyone, drinking his own at a gulp. Dick Barle winked at his mates, tipping the contents of his own glass into that of the landlord's.

A dark man, thin and swarthy, feared by both friends and enemies, Dick Barle cared for no one but himself. The other men followed his lead. After tossing off the four drinks, Freddy looked at his glass and seemed astonished to find it empty. He refilled the glasses with an unsteady hand, grinning cheerfully at the three men. Dick frowned; he was anxious to play cards with his almost drunk host. Pulling out a dirty pack from his pocket, he called, "Come on, lads, look for luck." George and Harry, his two friends, drew chairs up to the table. Harry laughed, saying, "That's right." He was a little dried-up man, with a sly face and tow-coloured hair. Everyone knew Harry Kell; he was an expert with the dogs, and spent all his spare time training them. His wife, to whom he had been married twelve years, told folks the only words he ever gave to her remarks were, "That's right." Dick and he usually worked together. The other man, young George Phips, sat down heavily, his thighs wide apart. He was flushed and nervous; he felt frightened. Only his hatred for Fred made him accept Dick's invitation to play at the Greyhound after hours. When they were all seated, Dick flashed round a hand of nap. By their prearranged agreement they played carelessly, allowing Fred to win when possible. Dick enjoyed himself thoroughly; he drew keen enjoyment from Fred's pleasure at winning. Every time the landlord won he winked slyly at George. While Dick attended to the cards Harry filled up the glasses. Freddy was dazed. At the next hand he picked up he looked unseeing at the cards with a grimace of disgust. "Sick of this game," he said thickly, throwing the hand down.

"Let's play banker." Dick nudged George, whispering, "Got him by the short hairs. Watch." Freddy leaned back, smiling at the miners in a friendly fashion. He was very happy. Ivy did not seem to understand that a man needed a little bit of sport at times. If she could only be reasonable, instead of darn silly. The collar he wore was too tight; leaning back in his chair he struggled vainly to release it from the stud. Dick nodded to Harry, who went to the landlord's assistance. When Freddy looked at the table again the cards were set in four neat packs. With a trembling hand he placed a ten shilling note on the pack nearest to the dealer. Nudging George with his knee Dick slid the pack up. It was the three of hearts. Fred's jaw fell; he waited for the banker's pack. It came, turned swiftly over, the ace of spades. Dick laughed coarsely; leaning over towards Fred he said, slowly, "You're drunk." Harry sniggered, "That's right."

Fred stared at them solemnly. He felt perfectly all right. Insulting him in his own home. Dirty, common miners, whom he only played with because there was no one else. Very slowly he asked, his voice clear, "Who says I'm drunk?" Dick snapped his fingers, recutting the pack. "I do." His friend's voice trailed in, "That's right." The room was filling with the fumes from Harry's pipe. Fred lurched to his feet; leaning towards Dick he said, "You're a liar. Come on, boys, drink up and have another." When Harry had said his say, George asked Dick doubtfully, "Won't do any harm, will it?" The banker looked surly: drink was the least important part of the game for the time being. When he had won all Fred's available money, he intended getting some of the bar stock too. He replied curtly, "Be quick then." The landlord took his glass eagerly from Harry, and emptied it at once. The banker asked him slyly, "How much money have you got now, Fred?" But Fred looked wise. "You wait an' see," he suggested. They played on. Fred still lost steadily. When twenty minutes had passed by, Dick repeated his question. Reaching for the whisky bottle, Fred poured himself another drink.

Dick and George watched him closely. Digging his hand down into his breeches pocket, he drew out a handful of small silver coins, which he counted clumsily. "Nine bob," with a leer he told them confidentially. "There was only three quid and some silver in little Tommy's store." Very carefully he piled the money on to a pack that Dick had already looked at, saying: "There you are. All I've got." Dick turned up the pack and held it under Fred's nose. It was a three of clubs. "You're out now," he sneered. "That's right," from Harry. The younger man flushed; he felt uncomfortable. If Fred were a fool, he, Dick and Harry were rogues. An impulse came to him to get up and tell his friends what he thought of them, but he was too frightened. Dick would put it all over the mine how he had funked and squealed. Besides, there was Clara. Fred was a swine who deserved far more than would ever come to him. He leaned forward, suggesting, "Stake that bottle of gin, Fred. Show 'em you're a good old sport." "I'm a sport, a good sport," Fred declared, trying to balance the bottle on a pack. Feeling suddenly miserable, George watched Dick slide an ace under the banker's pile; he was getting drunk himself. Bottle after bottle of the spirit stock was gained by Dick's method of play. Suddenly George realised that Harry was drunk, very drunk. There was only Dick left sober. For some reason that George could not fathom Fred refused to stake the one bottle of brandy. When the cigarettes and tobacco had all been lost to Dick, Fred commenced to gamble with the clothes he wore. Each garment won, Dick made its late owner strip off. By his side and under the table lay the things he had won. At last Fred possessed only his shirt and the bottle of brandy. The feeling of cold began to sober him. It would serve Ivy right for interfering. She should have minded her own business and let him have a bit of fun in a proper manner. Dick was determined to have both shirt and brandy; he intended to visit the Greyhound on Sunday night clad in Fred's clothes. It would be a grand joke. When he told them in the mine, they'd roar with laughter. George and Harry both being drunk, there would be no argument when he came to split up the gains. If only the world were full of such mugs he would be happy. Swifter than mining and better sport was banker if played cunningly. Young George was moody. The drink always turned him funny-like.

Grinning Dick looked round. Harry would need helping home. The night air would soon pull young George up stiff. How the villagers would chuckle when they knew of Fred's fall. There was still the shirt and brandy to get. "Come on, sport," he persuaded. "Shirt or brandy? Which or both against a quid or two?" "Brandy," said Fred. He held the bottle on a pack by the neck.

George, staring away at the door, saw it open.

Ivy came in; her hair had been bundled up quickly. Over her night-gown was a tweed skirt. She held a blanket, shawlways across her shoulders. She looked round the room, then gasped, "Fred!" Her husband snarled, "What's up with you?" while he watched Dick turn a low card from under the brandy bottle. "Damn!" he said loudly, for out of his own pack the banker showed a queen. Ivy clasped her hands; she was frightened badly. Fred there, half naked, with these beastly cheating miners. Earnestly she pleaded, "You'll ruin us, Fred. I could hear the row upstairs." Harry came out of his stupor with, "That's right." Very curtly Dick ordered him, "Shut up, you fool." Ivy continued, her voice plaintive, beseeching. "If the police caught us we'd lose the licence." Fred shouted, "Don't be a damn fool." Her finding him beaten infuriated him. "Can't I have a few friends in for a drink, eh?" "Friends," echoed Ivy, bitterly, breaking down. "Friends. Oh, Fred, can't you see? They've cheated you. Cheated you right and left, you fool."

She went to the foot of the stairs and called "Tom."

Ruth crouched on the landing. The noise from the room below had wakened her long since. She had been a fool to stay at a place like the Greyhound. Roy was, as usual, quite right. When Ivy left her bedroom, Ruth came out too. She did not wish them to see her or to know that she was there. The Greyhound people were, she could see, in for a terrible time. And if Roy was right, ultimate ruin lay ahead. Poor wretches. She heard Tom go into the smoke-room from the bar and tell Ivy, "He's found it." As she crept down the stairs the better to hear, she heard Ivy's voice ask, "The money?" The boy answered solemnly, his voice dull: "Yes." Ruth could see him. He wore an overcoat. She saw Dick plant the cards in three packs. His face was set hard and arrogant, Ivy and Tom he ignored.

"My quid to your shirt?" he asked. Fred nodded. He would teach Ivy a lesson.

Tom moved round to Dick's left hand and Fred was on his right. They watched him keenly. This time Dick knew he must play straight. Glaring contemptuously at his fuddled friends, he cut the cards. Fred won, turning up the queen of diamonds. He glanced round at Ivy, but she sat weeping, her head down. Feeling his luck was back, he staked the pound against his coat, and won it back. Dick was furious, wishing that he had ended the game ten minutes earlier. If only Harry and George were sober they could have kept a space clear round him so that he could have cheated unseen. The next game won back for Fred his bottle of brandy. He asked Tom for a drink. The boy gave him one grimly. The mood Fred was in he recognised as a dangerous one. It would be fatal to oppose him till the game was over. Tom had wild dreams that his brother-in-law might win back all that he had lost. Dick set the cards out swiftly, hoping to evade Tom's watchfulness. Unless he cleaned Fred right out, his story would not be worth the telling. The ace of spades lay ready to slide under his own pack; he took it up without a glance down. Tom saw him. "Cheat!" he shouted. "Look out, Fred!" Quickly Fred snatched up his stake money and Dick's.

The recent drink and his success made him exultant. He grinned at Dick, waving the two pound notes and said, "Mine; you'll have to be a bit smarter, mate." Clad in his coat and shirt, his face flushed and his hair towsled, he was a ludicrous figure. Ruth, watching, was anxious that he should win for the sake of his wife and brother-in-law. The game went on. Ruth was too interested in it to look at Ivy or the miners. A sudden scurry of air came round her naked ankles. Surely there was a door open somewhere. Drawing the brocade coat closely around her, she stared into the dark passage. She was suddenly cold. Someone was coming. She drew back into the shadows, hoping to remain unseen.

Clara, the barmaid, walked past, her head in the air.

The girl marched into the smoke-room, pushing the door wide open. She stared round the littered room and took it all in, the drunken George and the weeping Ivy, Fred's triumph and Tom's hard white face.

They seemed in a dream, not noticing her.

Snatching off her hat, she threw it on the card table. Dick brushed it angrily out of his way and looked up. They were all conscious of her then. Ivy, her head lifted, staring; Fred, in foolish amazement, a smile for her hovering round his weak mouth; George, gazing as though she were a spectre, and Tom unmoved.

Ivy's face was strained. She was listening.

With a wild laugh Clara advanced on Fred. "A visitor to see you, Mister blasted Flack, a visitor." P.C. Gaunter walked heavily up the passage, followed by Mrs. Tapin. He saw Ruth and taking her arm firmly led her into the lighted smoke-room. "This way, if you please, Miss," he said. Ruth laughed. Was she under arrest? How absurd! What did they do in such cases? Roy would laugh. From her side it was comedy, for the Flacks tragedy. Gaunter stood in the doorway, noting everyone and everything. He said civilly, taking out his note-book, "'Evening, all."

Ruth laughed inside. What a greeting for such a night! She looked at her watch. Ten minutes to twelve.

Fred looked up. A policeman. There was something wrong about that. He must be very decent, friendly, make the man like him. "'Evening, officer," he began, "'evening, old sport. Have a drink?" He held out a bottle of whisky invitingly, a foolish smile on his face. Ivy stared at him, a pang in her heart; he only looked a boy. Poor Freddy, silly lad. Then her heart hardened. He was a fool. He had ruined them all, wantonly. Her money would all go in clearing up the mess he had made by his manner of conducting the Greyhound. All Tom's struggling work, all her own hopes destroyed, for ever. She thought aloud, "My God, we're done now!" Ruth turned, gazing in pity. "Poor wretches," she thought. The constable spoke to her. "Now, Miss, your name and address, if you please." She gave it him, her voice steady, while her heart thumped. "Ruth Dorme, The Bristol Hotel, London." Looking at Tom, she saw him start at the familiar name.

Of them all, only the policeman remained stolid and unperturbed. Tom remembered Naxi. He need not have kept it from Ivy; she would be able to stand it now, one more horrid trick played on her. He crossed over to her, placing his arm round her shoulders. She still wept noiselessly, the tears hurrying down her face, her lips quivering. "Dear," he whispered, tenderly, "Naxi has gone. He . . . he is dead." Ivy looked up into his face, unable to speak, her hand pressing his, drawing love from the contact. Tom sighed; the problem of his own money keeping the Greyhound going was over now. As far as Freddy was concerned he would never be able to get another licence. Hard lines on Ivy, but so was everything. Ivy, poor kid. Why had she got to suffer for Freddy's mischief? If she could be persuaded to leave Freddy when they gave the Greyhound over. But Tom knew she would not do that; she would stay by her husband's side, suffering his defeats, an endless futility of vain hopes. Fred would never alter; he possessed no desire to.

The Tapins, mother and daughter, were by the wall near George Phips. Clara stared in malicious enjoyment of the Flacks' ruin. Standing there, her eyes hard and spiteful, like a mean child that has betrayed its playmates, she gloated on her victims. The villagers would treat her with respect after this. She had got back at all of them now.

While no one looked, Mrs. Tapin collected the untouched glass of whisky from under George's chair. She drank it quietly; no one but Ruth noticed her. After Clara's story had so upset her, she drank a quartern bottle of gin, while her daughter went out in search of P.C. Gaunter. Putting on her outdoor clothes she set out up the lane; reaching the top, where she could watch the Greyhound window lights, she waited for Clara and the policeman to come. So she felt quite chilly and the whisky under George's chair was a very welcome find. She looked round hopefully, but failed to discover any more. Clara was a clever girl—Mrs. Tapin smiled—in spite of her slip she was clever. Her own little trouble was best revealed to the villagers at the same time as the Greyhound scandal. The importance of one would help the more ordinary occurrence to lose its spice for them. When the inn trouble was set straight, folk would find Clara's scandal rather flat.

Nudging the slumbering George with her sharp elbow she roused him. Gaunter took the miners' names and addresses, then hers and Clara's.

Mrs. Tapin snivelled, she dabbed her eyes with a scrap of dirty white rag, rocking to and fro. In clumsy sympathy George put out his large hand, patting her bowed shoulders gently.

Presently Mrs. Tapin started to tell him of Clara's trouble. She told her story artfully, laying all the blame on Flack's shoulders. George listened bitterly; at the end he started up violently in the direction of the landlord. When he saw the blue uniform of the police constable his raised fist dropped. No good going against the law. He was in enough trouble as it was. The magistrates would fine him for certain. There would be a day lost from work in the mines. A bright thought cheered his brain. He turned to Mrs. Tapin, nodding at Clara. "I'll still take her," he said firmly. The girl laughed harshly. Putting her head down on a level with George's she sneered, "Take me? You wait till you're asked, which won't be ever." She laughed again loudly. George sunk his head forward, hiding his face. No one must see his tears. Tom, too, was near to weeping; his money could not save them now.

Police Constable Gaunter shut his note-book and put it away. He had obtained all the information he required. He made the miners and Mrs. Tapin and her daughter leave the inn. When they had gone, he said "Good night," in a hard voice; only Ruth answered him, then he too went. Ruth crept out after him. She felt tired and unhappy. The world was large and she had stumbled accidentally on a patch of human misery. There did not seem anything that she could do to help. It was like encountering a cripple; nothing one said, did or thought made the slightest difference.

Roy would be round to fetch her in the morning. If Roy asked her again—he would—she would marry him. She went into the dark bedroom and, without lighting her candle, slid into bed. Soon she would sleep.

Tom went out and bolted the heavy door. Thank God they had all gone. Ivy and Fred still sat there in silent despair. The boy knew their icy thoughts, their futile regrets. He gazed at them; they sat still. Why did they stay there? Poor things. They should be upstairs in bed, fast asleep. For him and for them life at the Greyhound was over. The few weeks of waiting till the law deposed them from the Greyhound would scarcely count; a negative period quickly forgotten.

In Grovelace woods the flowers would bloom, anemones, bluebell flowers, the trees put out their young leaves . . . he would not see. . . . Yet he would know them there. . . . He could be brave, help his brother and sister on towards another finer goal. In a year, this night's sorrow would be a scar on memory, nothing more.

Suddenly Tom felt tired; he yawned unwillingly. Looking at his watch he yawned again.

They had reached the day's end.

THE END